The Island Expats Book 1
(New Beginnings)
By Deb McEwan

Cover Design by Jessica Bell

In loving memory of
Andy Kirby
29 December 1950 to 24 December 2020
Taken too soon

The Island Expat series is set on the island of Souvia,
shown on the map above.

Chapter 1 – England

Matt woke up in a sweat and felt the panic invade his whole body.

The image in his mind was as clear as the day it had happened, some two years before. He was lying on the floor, right leg twisted, looking at a mangled body in the distance, one arm missing and recognisable as a female only by the hair that he'd seen when the girl had been sitting opposite him earlier, her legs up on the seat beside her. Some of that hair was now singed but she would have been more bothered about the state of her body, he thought, rather than her hair.

Then he remembered what the therapist had told him. Despite his heart beating like a sparrow's when trying to escape from a cat, Matt pushed the images and thoughts from his mind and concentrated on his breathing. Deep breaths; slowly in through his nose and out through his mouth. Each time an image or thought tried to invade the calm, he imagined he was pushing it away, and eventually, his heart rate slowed to its regular rhythm and the panic subsided.

Now feeling much better, Matt looked around. It was pitch black and he couldn't see a thing. He lifted his arm and looked at the time on the fitness monitoring watch on his wrist; 2:15. Dog tired, but worried the horrors would recur if he went back to sleep, Matt spoke to his Echo.

'Alexa, play my favourite music.'

Alexa lit up and the sounds of the eighties soon filled the room. Matt sang along quietly to *Eye of the Tiger* before reaching over to pick up the book he was currently reading about the island. He was due to visit the following week, having talked a few ex-copper mates into accompanying him on a long weekend of golf. He also planned to see Elena, the other, much more pleasant, image he often woke up to these days, and would stay on after his friends left. He put the book down. If those hazel eyes and that smile weren't enough, her dry sense of humour and refreshing, straightforward knack for telling it as it is did the trick, and he found himself smiling again, just thinking about her.

After an indeterminate amount of time, Matt felt his eyelids closing and turned off the music before falling asleep. When he awoke again it was daylight, but when he looked out of the window, people were rushing by in the street below, umbrellas up, trying not to let the drizzle soak them to the skin.

Had he not already made a commitment to the local dog shelter, Matt would have been tempted to curl up downstairs with a coffee, toast, and his book. He laughed. 'Who are you trying to kid?' he asked himself, before getting up and doing his morning stretches so his joints and muscles were fluid, which meant he could walk to the bathroom without being in pain. Patience was another thing he'd had to learn since the accident and it was as hard to master as was overcoming his physical injuries.

A hurried shower, a rushed coffee and a ten-minute drive took him to the shelter where he said a quick hello to the other volunteers before making his way to the pen that Jenny shared with another dog. He heard the Golden Retriever/Border Collie/Heinz 57 cross-breed – well, that's what they told him she was – before seeing her.

'Hello, my friend,' he said, and after Jenny got over her initial excitement at seeing Matt, she sat in front of him with her head down as Matt stroked and cuddled her, 'aren't you a beautiful girl?' he asked and Jenny's tailed thumped happily on the ground as Matt continued to tell her how special she was. Eventually satisfied with the attention, Jenny stood up and shook herself, indicating it was time for Matt to take her for a walk. A few of the other volunteers gave an indulgent shake of their heads and smiled. Most other dogs wanted to go for a walk straight away and Jenny was the only one who liked so much attention first. Neither man nor beast was bothered about the rain, and as they walked through the deserted local woods, Matt explained to the dog about how the terrors had woken him again in the middle of the night.

'I suppose it's the equivalent of you being chased by devil dogs,' he told her as she squatted for a pee. But she was still looking at him as if she were listening. The logical side of Matt's brain told him that he was as daft as a brush and if anyone saw him they'd think he was twenty sandwiches short of a picnic. The old Matt, who hadn't let the sights he'd seen for his first twenty-eight years in the police force affect his mental health, would have agreed wholeheartedly, but this new guy, who had been struggling with demons since the train crash two years earlier, now knew that he had to do whatever he could to keep it together. And as bizarre as it might have seemed to his old self, he believed this dog knew he was damaged and had made it her job to help him get better.

The horrors hadn't been as bad since he'd started volunteering at the rescue centre – Matt had already completed the paperwork required to adopt Jenny and the manager was happy that the pair were a good fit for each other. It was just a matter of time now, and when he returned from the island he planned to bring her home for good.

'Do you want to come and live with me, Jen?' he asked, and the dog replied by wagging her tail and doing that thing with her eye that looked to Matt as if she was winking at him. The manager at the centre had just shaken her head and laughed when he mentioned it to her and laughed, so Matt had kept it to himself ever since.

This last walk before he was due to be away for a week was longer than the others, and Matt felt that Jenny sensed something was different. 'I know you'll miss me, and I'll miss you too,' he said, as he brushed Jenny when they returned from their walk. 'But it's only for a week and then you're coming to live with me. And I'll never abandon you. I promise.'

He said a final goodbye to the dog who had already helped to save his life and made his way home. Matt knew that Jenny was already a big part of his life and, however his relationship progressed with Elena, they would come as a package.

Chapter 2

After the initial banter and a few drinks on the three and a half hour flight, the men settled down. They ate their pre-ordered meals, then Bob and Keith closed their eyes, intending to doze during the rest of the journey. Wary of sleeping in any public places, Matt took out his book and read a little more about Souvia. Elena's four-star hotel was situated towards the west of the island, was well reported, and had received mostly five-star reviews on Trip Advisor and other websites. Matt wasn't surprised; Elena was a smart, intelligent woman, and he already knew that she was business-savvy.

Theirs had been a chance meeting, and while the others slept, he let himself daydream, recalling the time they'd met and how their relationship had progressed…

It was a miserable October morning and was tipping down with rain. Matt was about to jump onto the pavement having just crossed the main town road when he'd heard a noise behind him and a woman's voice using some colourful language. When he turned around, a woman was trying to retrieve items of shopping back into a supermarket bag that had broken, and the contents were strewn on the ground. The green pedestrian crossing light had started flashing and then turned from green to red, and some impatient drivers were already sounding their horns. Matt stopped to help her, and by the time they took shelter under a shop gazebo on the pavement, they were both dripping wet.

'Thanks for your help,' she said with a weak smile, attempting to wipe the rain from her forehead. 'You'd think I'd know better by now and I'd be prepared for the weather in this country. So why is it a surprise every time I flaming well visit?'

'You're not from here?' Matt asked. Looking at the woman in front of him who was dripping wet, struggling with an inadequate umbrella and trying to organise her shopping, he couldn't help himself and chuckled out loud.

'This is funny?' she asked, but her lips started twitching too and they both burst into gales of laughter. 'I hope I don't look as bad as I think I do?' she said after they calmed down.

Matt simply nodded. He hadn't had such a good laugh in ages and it lifted his spirits, despite the greyness of the day. He liked this woman already and didn't even know her. Out of nowhere, Matt heard himself taking the plunge. 'Look,' he said. 'There's a pub just around the corner from here, the Red Lion. Shall we go there, dry off and have a drink and something to eat?'

He thought he'd blown it when he saw the face that had been smiling a few seconds before, turn deadly serious.

'Sorry, it was just a suggestion. I thought you'd want to dry off…'

'It was a good suggestion, too,' she replied, smiling again. 'And yes, that would be great, thanks.'

Although never sure whether offers of help would be taken the wrong way by some women, Matt decided he would ask anyway, already feeling that he wanted to do anything he could to help this particular woman. 'I can help with your bag if you like? Until you get yourself sorted,' he added, just in case she took it the wrong way.

'That's kind, thanks.'

Matt picked up the shopping bag and tucked it under his arm. 'Ready,' he asked and she followed him as they left cover and ran to the pub around the corner.

Matt ordered a pot of tea for two and took off his wet raincoat while she went to sort herself out. The bedraggled woman who'd entered the ladies emerged as a smart and tidied version of herself. Her damp hair was now lying tidily in shoulder-length curls and she'd reapplied her pale red lipstick which emphasised her very kissable lips against her wrinkle-free pale olive skin. He resisted the urge to say, *'You scrub up well,'* and smiled as she approached the booth. 'Better?' he asked.

5

'Much, and thanks again for your help. I'm Elena,' she said and held out a hand for Matt to shake.

'Matt, and glad to be of service.'

Elena sat down and made herself comfortable. 'I don't make a habit of taking tea and spending time with men I've only just met,' she said. 'Just so you know.'

Matt laughed. 'And I don't make a habit of inviting women I've just met to come to the pub with me either. So now we've got that sorted, would you like something to eat, or just the tea?'

'We might as well have a bite to eat now that we're here, and you can tell me a bit about yourself.'

Two hours later, after they'd finished eating and progressed on to having a proper drink, they were still laughing and talking when Elena's phone buzzed. She fished it out of her bag.

'Good grief is that the time?' she asked as she read the message. 'I really must get going. My father wants to know if I'm still alive.' She explained that she was visiting England with her father and they were combining business with visits to his elderly parents. 'Thanks so much for your help today.'

'Think nothing of it,' Matt said, already wondering if he would see her again.

They both hesitated. Elena was the first to break the silence. 'My family are having a big get-together tonight before Dad flies home tomorrow. Do you fancy it?'

Oh yes, definitely. 'Are you sure? I wouldn't want to intrude…'

Her expression changed at his words and Matt realised Elena might think it was a brush-off. 'But I'd love to come if you're sure.'

'That's settled then.' She smiled again and those hazel eyes twinkled. 'Eight o'clock at the Athena restaurant. See you there?'

'You certainly will, Elena.'

She put some money down on the table to pay her half of the bill and Matt knew better than to argue. He hoped there'd be plenty of occasions he could treat her in the future.

'Laters,' she said with a smile before disappearing out of the pub.

The Athena was the only Greek restaurant in town and Matt had eaten there a few times with some of his work colleagues. They'd had his farewell dinner there when he left the police force; the demons had been bad then and he could barely remember turning up for it, but recalled leaving as soon as he could.

This time he was a little early, so had a drink at the bar while he waited. Soon after he'd told the barman that he was waiting for Elena, the owner turned up for a chat.

'Nice to see you again, Mr Elliott,' the man said, holding out his hand to shake, and Matt was impressed that he remembered his name.

'It's Matt,' he said, 'and good to be here.'

'Panikos,' the man said as they shook hands. 'And what's your association with Elena and her family?' The smile on his face didn't reach his eyes.

Matt was taken aback at the directness of his question, but didn't show it. 'We're friends, and look, here she is now,' he said, and could see that the restaurateur wasn't best pleased with his response. Matt stood as Elena approached the bar.

'Hello,' she said, kissing Matt on both cheeks.

Panikos hurried from behind the bar to the front and was standing in front of Elena before Matt could say abracadabra. He stood in front of Matt's barstool with his back to him and held Elena's shoulders. He said something in Greek that Matt didn't understand, then kissed her on both cheeks.

'You look beautiful, my sweet,' he said, after the greeting, and Matt sensed that this was as much for his benefit as it was for Elena's. Matt looked down, feigning disinterest, but Panikos had got under his skin and he didn't like the man.

'Thank you, Panni,' Elena replied. 'Matt, Panni and I are old friends and went to school together before going our separate ways.'

Oh, really?

'Our families are close and it's always good to see each other for a catch up. Shall we sit down? Usual table, Panni?'

Matt tried to hide his smile at the way she'd dismissed her *old friend,* who didn't look best pleased, as Elena led the way to the table and both men followed.

'I've put your grandmother next to you, Elena, and I thought your new friend could sit next to your grandmother. Then your father and the boys–'

'That's really kind, Panni, but I know how busy you are, so I'll sort out the seating. What delights have you got for us this evening?'

Matt made a mental note that Elena was masterful at getting her own way and her charm and smile could lessen the blow. He noticed that it hadn't had the desired effect in this case as Panni gave him an unhappy look first before stomping to the bar and raising his voice as he said something in Greek to the barman.

'Are you happy to sit here, Matt?' she asked, then winked discreetly at him.

So, he had nothing to worry about as far as Panni was concerned. Matt sat down and Elena sat next to him. 'Expect a grilling tonight, but I'm sure you can handle it.'

Before he had a chance to reply there was lots of noise from the door and they both looked in that direction. A man headed up the front of a group of people, along with an older woman who had her arm linked through his. Two young men followed. They had Elena's mouth and it was obvious they were her twin sons. They were followed by another man and woman of around Matt's age, he guessed, and a twenty-something man and woman who were holding hands. They all headed for the table but the twins stopped in mid-walk when they noticed him sitting next to their mother. In unison, they looked towards Panni, who was standing behind the bar, to Matt, then

8

directly at their mother. It almost looked like a rehearsed sketch show scene. Matt resisted the urge to fold his arms and frown. Almost thirty years as a detective had trained his poker face, so instead of displaying his true feelings, he plastered a smile on his face, showing a welcome that he didn't particularly feel.

He was relieved that most of the party were smiling genuinely and warmly as they headed towards the table, but the twins weren't and they moved faster, arriving first.

'Hi,' one of them said. 'We haven't met.'

Matt held out his hand. 'Matt Elliott. Good to meet you.'

'I'm Nick,' the twin said as they shook hands.

'And I'm Andy,' the other said, holding out his hand. They were then silent, trying to faze him, Matt thought, as he looked from one to the other. The boys looked away first, almost at the same time. Even though he was used to his own twins being in sync with each other's thoughts, he wasn't used to seeing two people who looked like clones of each other, their movements synchronised without having to talk about it. It was both fascinating and disorienting.

Andy was wearing black chinos and Nick's were grey, so Matt made a mental note to spot the difference that way.

'How do you two know each other?' Nick asked.

'Your mother and I met…'

'Matt and I are friends, darling,' Elena said, 'and he's joining us for dinner tonight so I'm sure there'll be plenty of time to give him the third degree between courses.'

'Mum!' Andy said, now sounding more like a teenager than a grown man. 'As if.'

'You must be Matt?' Elena's father and grandmother had now arrived at the table and Matt turned his attention to them while the twins found their seats and made themselves comfortable. 'I'm Jim Lacey,' her father said, pumping Matt's hand vigorously. 'This is my mum, Victoria, and if you think you're going to get the third degree from the twins, just wait until she starts!' Jim laughed heartily and Matt smiled as he said hello to Elena's grandmother, before being introduced to her aunt, uncle, niece and niece's boyfriend.

Introductions made, they settled down and made some small talk, Matt telling Elena about his twins before Jim jumped into the conversation.

'I'm going home tomorrow,' he said, 'and Elena's staying to represent the family interests, and also to spend some time with the twins and her grandmother of course, before leaving next week. I wish I could be with her to meet with Rob Green, but my wife is due to have an operation and I promised I'd be there.'

Elena's face fell and Matt assumed she was worried about her mother. 'I'm sorry to hear that your wife isn't well,' he said. 'I hope she makes a full recovery.'

'I'm sure she will, Matt, it's a routine op on her arm that she's been waiting for, for some time.'

'I see.' He didn't.

The conversation moved on as Matt wondered what was bothering Elena. The first meze courses arrived and they all got stuck into the halloumi, lounza and then vine leaves filled with delicious delicacies.

'What do you do, Matt?' Victoria asked, in between mouthfuls. The others at the table stopped talking as all eyes fell on him. He felt like he was at an interview.

'I'm an ex-detective and retired last year.'

'And do you work now?'

'Yes, I have my own consultancy business,' Matt replied. He popped a piece of the tasty halloumi cheese into his mouth—he hadn't accepted any new cases for the past two months, but still had his business, so it was only stretching the truth.

'And what rank were you when you retired?'

'For goodness sake, Nanna! You'll be shining a light on Matt any second now. Can we change the subject please?'

The others laughed and it was the turn of the twins to get the third degree from their grandmother as she asked if they were working hard and how their courses were going. 'Your grandfather would have done something in the sports world if he'd had the opportunity,' she said. 'So I expect great things from you both.'

Matt could see from the twins' expressions that this wasn't the first time they'd heard this from their grandmother so he decided to change the subject.

'What's your hotel like?' he asked, and Elena's face lit up as her father started talking.

'The building had been in Maria's family for years before we married. It was always our dream to make it better and we decided to do a rebuild some ten years ago and also to enlarge it.'

'It was a massive undertaking,' Elena interrupted, 'and Dad and Mum made many sacrifices during the years to be able to achieve what we have now. For the first time in ages, it's actually making a profit and…'

'Elena, I'm sure Matt doesn't want to know all of our problems.'

'Sorry, Dad, but I'm so proud of all that you've achieved, I can't help showing off about it. We had a bit of a setback due to the virus, but so did everyone else in our industry.'

'We've come through it, though,' Jim said. 'Better than most and the future's looking bright. Maybe you should visit, Matt?'

Matt sensed that they were being overly optimistic about their past problems but didn't expect to be told anything further. It was his first outing with Elena – he wasn't sure whether to call it a date – and he hadn't expected to find out so much about her and her family business so soon. His train of thought made him realise he expected to see her again and he stopped himself and concentrated on answering her father's question.

Everyone stopped talking as they waited for his response.

'That sounds like a plan, Jim,' he said, non-committedly. They seemed satisfied by his answer and continued eating.

The group were talking amongst themselves and it gave Matt a chance to enjoy himself with Elena.

'Is your hotel in the middle of the…'

'Everything all right?' Panni seemed to appear from nowhere and he asked the question.

Matt folded his arms and looked at the restaurateur. 'The food is excellent thank you, Panni. Absolutely delicious.'

Panni nodded, gave a tight smile and left them to it.

'In the middle of the tourist area,' Matt continued, ignoring the food and leaning towards Elena.

'It's not far from the main tourist town, Matt. We…'

'More wine?' A bottle appeared in between them with Panni attached to it, and then he moved forward, placing himself between them so Matt had to lean back.

'Our glasses are still full, Panni, but thanks anyway,' Matt said, trying his best not to laugh. Elena couldn't help herself and when Panni left the table this time, she giggled.

Matt looked towards their host who was now at the table next to theirs, squirting cleaning solution onto it and rigorously wiping it down with a cloth. He leaned towards Elena. 'I'm sure your hotel is wonderful and who knows, maybe I'll get to see it one day.'

'I hope so, Matt.'

The moment was broken by the sound of the cleaning solution bottle dropping to the floor.

'Ooops,' Matt said, as he turned to Panni and shrugged his shoulders.

Panni's face reddened and he looked away from Matt and made his way to the bar.

'I think he might leave us alone now,' Elena said as the waiters kept the courses coming and Matt had to stop eating before he exploded. By the time they'd finished, he was satisfied that Elena had no romantic interest in her old friend, despite Panni's obvious behaviour for it to be otherwise. The twins hadn't yet warmed to him but he could understand that they only had their mother's best interests at heart and wasn't particularly bothered – yet. Hell, he didn't even know if they would see each other again.

As the evening wound up, Jim asked for the bill and went to the bar with his wallet to pay it. Matt jumped up and joined him, insisting on paying his own way, despite the protestations from Elena's father, who eventually acquiesced.

'Are you ready, Mum?' Nick asked Elena a few minutes later, and yet again, everyone stopped what they were doing and looked at Elena and Matt.

'Almost,' she said. 'If you all go and say goodbye to Panni, I'll meet you outside in a few minutes.'

They said their goodbyes to Matt with Andy adding, 'Good to meet you, Matt. Will we be seeing you again?'

Jim laughed at his grandson's attempt to garner more information.

'Good to meet you too, and I hope so.' Matt replied, as much for Panni's benefit as for the family.

'Now then, Panni…' Jim said, putting an around the host as he started walking towards the door, giving Panni no choice but to go with him.

Elena and Matt were left at the table on their own.

'That was delicious thanks,' Matt said. 'And very interesting. I feel as grilled as the halloumi cheese.'

She laughed. 'Would it be too forward of me to ask if we could meet up again before I go?'

'I'd like that,' he said, now serious. 'Are you free for dinner tomorrow?'

'I have meetings scheduled all day but that would be a lovely end to a busy day.'

They made the arrangements and, forgetting for a moment that all eyes were on him, Matt lifted Elena's hand and kissed it. They smiled at each other as if they were the only two people in the restaurant.

The sound of smashing glass broke the mood followed by Panni saying, 'Oops.' He watched Elena and her new man burst into spontaneous laughter, and he knew at that moment that he'd lost any chance of the relationship he desired with his childhood friend.

13

Matt knew straight away that something was wrong as soon as Elena walked into *The Silver Gate* the following night. He watched as the Maître'd welcomed her and noticed that the charming man didn't raise a smile from Elena. She did smile when she saw him but her hazel eyes didn't sparkle like they had the night before. Matt started to feel insecure, and was annoyed at himself for feeling that way.

He stood as she arrived at the table and they kissed a greeting on each cheek. Matt was relieved that Elena seemed genuinely pleased to see him as the Maître'd pulled back her chair with a flourish and she sat down. When the man left them to it to study the menu, Matt took the plunge. 'You look lovely, Elena.'

Her eyes sparkled at the compliment. 'Thanks, Matt, you don't brush up too badly either.'

'Aw shucks,' he said. 'Go, on with you.'

They laughed and chatted about the previous night as the waiter arrived with the wine Matt had requested, and then took their order. Although wondering why she wasn't as bright as she had been the day before, Matt didn't want to pressure Elena, so decided to wait to see if she would confide in him.

Halfway through the melon and Parma ham starters, she put down her cutlery and sighed. 'I've had a terrible day.'

'I thought something was up, Elena. What happened?'

'We needed some financial assistance for the hotel after such a dreadful year and Dad's decided to go to a private investor, instead of a bank.'

'And you don't approve?'

'I approve of the sentiment and the lower interest rate, but not of the individual. Dad knows the family and liked the investor's father, so he approves of them. But I don't like Rob Green, Matt. As soon as I met him I had a gut instinct that something was off.' She leaned forward and almost whispered, 'It's taken me a while, but after forty-eight years of living on this planet, I've learnt to trust my gut instincts.'

'I couldn't agree more–and you look younger than forty-eight by the way.'

'Oh, you smoothie,' Elena said, then gave him that smile that lit up her whole face.

Matt was glad it had the desired effect, but was concerned for her. 'What's the solution? Your father seems a good judge of character to me. Can you get him to change his mind?'

'I did try but he said we have to act with our heads as far as this is concerned, not our hearts, and go for the best deal.'

'I see. What do you know about Rob Green?'

'His father made money in the recycling business, but not until Rob was in his late teens as far as I'm aware. He was an adult when his father died suddenly of a heart attack. I believe he used some of that money to invest in various projects and seems to be quite canny as far as those investments are concerned. He's part-owner of the Marlborough Hotel and Golf Resort which is a few minutes' drive from our hotel. Guests who visit on golf holidays often stay at our hotel as it's a less expensive alternative. I think he has his finger in a number of pies and his money works for him, so he doesn't need to do much. He's quite rough around the edges and I wouldn't like to be alone in a room with him.'

'Ah, I see…'

'But saying that, Matt, there's a lot of people I wouldn't like to be alone with.'

They both laughed then Matt asked, 'Do you need to have much to do with him? As long as you make the repayments on time, can't your contact be mostly by phone or email?'

'That would be ideal yes. But Rob loves his golf. I believe his wife spends most of her time on the island where they have a stunning villa near Souva, the capital. Instead of staying there when he plays golf, Rob has decided he wants to stay at our modest hotel occasionally when he visits, so it's not that simple I'm afraid.'

Matt nodded.

'I intend to trust my instincts and will do my best not to give the man any opportunities to test my judgement.'

The waiter came to take away their plates and topped up the wine glasses. Elena smiled her thanks then turned back to Matt. 'Now, can we talk about you for a while?'

'I'm divorced and single, Elena, and you know that I have twins, too. My daughter, Kayleigh, is an adrenaline junkie and works for an adventure holiday tour company. She's currently taking a group of tourists up Kilimanjaro before going to work in Majorca. My son, Glen, is a sport psychologist. He's doing his PhD while working for the physical rehab department of the General Hospital in York. He hopes to eventually work for one of the top-flight rugby league clubs, but knows he'll have to work his way up to that.'

'You must be very proud of them both.'

'I am, yes. They've done well for themselves and we all get along well. What about your boys?'

'I'm proud of them too and glad they're settled at Uni. Their father's a chauvinist and a difficult man, but that's another story. Anyway, I had to work really hard to make sure the boys grew up into responsible men who respect women. And I feel quite fortunate that they've turned out the way they have. Some of our earlier experiences mean they're a bit over-protective of me.'

'I did notice, yes,' Matt said, raising an eyebrow.

Elena laughed. 'I can't complain though, Matt.'

The main course arrived and they took a moment to savour the food before Elena continued, 'Have you been divorced for long?'

'Six years, but we lived separate lives long before that. Sally's remarried now and the kids tell me she's happy, so I'm glad about that.'

They carried on eating and chatting and, towards the end of the meal, Elena explained that she was staying at her grandmother's.

'…if I don't get back at a reasonable hour she just worries. But tomorrow I have a meeting with the parent company of a supplier that we use. It's in London and I'm going to stay over. I wondered if you'd care to join me, if you're not too busy? Perhaps we can spend the following day seeing some sights?'

'I think I can manage that,' Matt replied. 'Let me know the name of the hotel and I'll book a room.'

'No need for that, Matt. There's plenty of room in mine.'

He leaned across and squeezed her hand. Both felt the electricity and anticipation running through their veins.

Chapter 3 – Souvia

As Matt, Bob, and Keith were settling down on their flight, Fiona Green was being entertained by a man a number of years her junior. They'd spent a wicked afternoon in a serviced apartment she rented on the far side of the island, almost a two-hour drive from Orchard Heights, the impressive villa she shared with her husband, Rob. For extra security and to protect her privacy, Fiona always used her Jane Smith email address and the same pseudonym to book the apartment. She left the payment in cash in an envelope on the side table next to the door. The first time she'd done this, the owner had wanted to meet her, to ensure that she handed over the money, but Fiona had insisted otherwise and offered almost twenty per cent over the quoted fee. Greed had won the day and the owner had decided to trust her. She also knew that cash payments were lucrative for islanders who would not then have to declare the earnings and could pocket the whole amount without having to pay tax.

Fiona was well aware that someone may be watching her movements, so she disguised herself as well as she could as she came and went from the apartment. She forgot about this as she looked at her lover as he jumped out of bed, heading towards the bathroom.

Stephen Goodman had his father's good looks and his mother's sense of humour, which meant he was charming, witty, and great fun to be around. He'd been spoilt as a youngster but now his parents had recognised the error of their ways and were trying to do something about it. Now in his mid-twenties, Stephen was having to find his own way in life and he was currently studying for a degree in hotel management and training as an assistant manager in the Griffon's Rest, towards the west of the island. Fiona knew he could sulk if he didn't get his own way, just like his mother, and she sensed he had her temper too, although Fiona hadn't yet experienced this. She had been on the wrong side of Sasha's temper more than a few times throughout the years, and hoped she knew how to handle the youngster, to avoid any temper tantrums. Looking at him as he returned from the bathroom, she felt some regret. It was a shame she had to end it, but Stephen was getting needy and serious and it was becoming boring. He loved the gifts she had given him but had also started asking for money, and Fiona was nobody's fool.

Here goes, she thought as he jumped back into bed. 'How's Leanne?' she asked, hoping that their engagement was about to be confirmed. Sasha had already told her that they were expecting Stephen and Leanne to marry, so Fiona hoped this would make her job easier. She should have known by now that life didn't always turn out as expected.

'Ah…'

'What do you mean, *ah*? What sort of answer is that?'

'I spoke to her earlier today. I meant to tell you as soon as I got here but then you didn't want to talk, so I thought it would keep.'

'Thought what would keep, Stephen? What on earth are you talking about?'

'I'm fed up with hiding our love, Fiona, and I know you feel the same, so I've…'

'Our love? What have you done?' Fiona felt her heart rate quicken and hoped her instincts were wrong.

'I told her I've met someone else and it's over between us. Then she asked me if the rumours were true. I know you didn't want to go public yet, so I didn't say a word but Leanne's not stupid and she's put two and two together… You know I'm mad about you and I want the whole world to know it.'

Fiona clenched the duvet, loosened her grip and clenched again. It did nothing to slow her heart rate and it took immense effort not to grab the nearest heavy object and bash Stephen with it until he stopped talking. She closed her eyes and took a deep breath. It took a will of iron to control her emotions and her voice.

'Fiona?'

'You stupid, stupid, idiot!'

19

'Fiona, what's wrong? You said you were going to leave Rob and we could be together and—'

'I didn't say any such thing! Why would I leave Rob for a glorified waiter, Stephen? Are you completely insane?' Fiona couldn't control herself anymore and jumped out of the bed. This would be all over the island in no time and she'd have a job explaining it to Rob and her friends.

'How could you be so stupid?' she asked. She picked up her phone and went into the bathroom, slamming the door behind her.

As soon as she took her phone off silent and *Do not disturb,* it pinged like pinging was going out of fashion. There were a number of messages from Sasha. The first simply said, *Call me.* That had been sent over two hours before and another six had arrived since. Fiona could tell that Sasha's temper had grown as time progressed as each message was ruder than the last. The penultimate message asked, *How could you do this to my family?* and the final message contained a number of expletives and ended with a threat.

Typical, Fiona thought, *it's always the woman who gets blamed and never the man.*

She took a shower, hoping that Stephen had got the message and would be gone by the time she'd finished. Fiona knew she had to control the damage and as the hot water refreshed her body, she started to formulate a plan. Feeling a lot calmer after drying herself and putting a luxurious robe around her, she returned to the bedroom. Stephen was dressed and sitting on the bed. His eyes looked swollen and he wiped a few tears from his face.

Good grief. She tried to put a sympathetic expression on her face. 'It was always a bit of fun, Stephen. You must know that, surely?'

'But I love you, Fiona! And I'm not a waiter, I'm a trainee manager.'

'I don't know why you feel like that. I've never given you the—'

'But when I talked to you about us being together you didn't say we wouldn't be. You led me on and–'

'Now you just wait a minute, Stephen. I've never said the words *I love you,* and I certainly haven't told you we were going to be together. This has always been a bit of fun for me. I told you that from the start and I thought you felt the same.'

'But when I said I loved you, you said, *Me too!*'

'That's nonsense, Stephen and you know it.'

'We were in this bed and we'd just made love. I said I love you and–'

'So you're holding me responsible for something I muttered under my breath before falling asleep? And on that basis you've dumped the girl your mother told me you were going to marry, and have probably ruined my reputation to boot? You're twenty-five years old, Stephen, and you're acting like a flaming teenager!'

'But I love you, Fiona!'

'And I love Rob!'

'You don't love Rob. And if he's out of the picture we could be together and–'

'I never want to see you again! Get out, Stephen. Now!'

Fiona started with the pillows, throwing them at him one by one. She unplugged the lamp and threw that, too, which Stephen managed to dodge. Her eyes flicked around the room in an attempt to find something suitable to inflict as much pain as she could.

Stephen had seen her mad before, but not this mad, and he knew that now wasn't the time to reason with her. He moved his head as the TV remote whizzed past it, then grabbed his bag, grateful that he'd shoved his phone, wallet, and electronic cigarette into the side pocket while she was still in the bathroom.

'We'll speak when you've calmed down,' he called from the door. 'Don't worry, Fiona, everything will be all right. When Rob's out of the picture we can–'

'Rob will never be out of the picture. It's over, you stupid pri…' she called, but the door had already closed

21

behind him. A few minutes later, her uncontrolled fury had turned to calm, seething anger. Her reputation could be in ruins because of Sasha's son but if Rob had paid her more attention she wouldn't have to go looking for it elsewhere. She packed her bag and looked around her. Fiona doubled the amount she usually left which would more than cover the damage.

Rob was back from his business trip to London and was planning on coming home tonight, instead of staying at the Griffon's Rest as he sometimes did. She knew it had been a risk, taking a lover that worked in the hotel where her husband stayed, but that had added to the excitement. Now it was a worry, and as she left and made her way home on the highway, her mind was working overtime.

She blamed her current situation on everyone but herself. There was no way she'd agree to a divorce if Rob found out what she'd been up to, and ensuring that he didn't was her number one priority. As she formulated a plan of action, Fiona had no idea that fate was about to solve some of her problems for her.

As the waiter carried the coffee laden tray towards the meeting room at the Griffon's Rest hotel, Leanne Carter bumped into him.

'You stupid…' The waiter stopped himself from muttering the expletives that were on the tip of his tongue.

'I'm sorry, Karl,' she said. 'It was an accident. You go and sort yourself out and I'll get some more. Which table?' She asked as if she didn't know.

Karl looked at her as if she had two heads. 'The small meeting room, Leanne, where I'm heading now.' He shook his head. 'The charming Mr Green and Mr Goodman.'

'Of course. I've got it.' She started picking up the mess from the floor and putting the items back on the tray. Thankfully, nothing was broken. She prepared a new tray in the kitchen where nobody could see her. The meeting room door was ajar and Leanne was about to enter when she heard voices and recognised them as belonging to the boss and Rob Green. She hesitated and listened.

'I'm not interested,' she heard Elena say.

'Come on, love. This way the loan will be paid off sooner and we'll have a bit of fun while we're at it.'

'My family may owe you money, Mr Green, but you are a slimy, good-for-nothing, sad excuse for a man and I wouldn't sleep with you if the future of the human race depended on it!'

Leanne heard him laugh.

'I like a challenge'.

'Coffee,' said Leanne, walking into the room and seeing the grateful look Elena sent her way. She put a cup in front of Rob Green and the other on the table next to some papers. Mr Goodman's jacket was hanging from the back of the empty chair beside it. 'Would you like anything else?' she asked.

'Serve them afternoon tea please, Leanne,' Elena said, adding, 'Goodbye, Mr Green.' She made the words sound like she'd just stood in something unpleasant.

Elena was furious. Yet again, she regretted not being firm enough with her father and insisting they get a proper bank loan instead of going through the slimy, good-for-nothing… She stopped this train of thought when she saw the stain on the light blue carpet.

'Dammit,' she said out loud as Leanne walked through the door with an empty tray. 'What happened here?' She stopped her waitress before she could go to the kitchen to order the food for the meeting. *He can damn well wait.*

'I bumped into Karl when he was taking the coffee in, sorry.' Leanne sighed. 'I was going to clear it up after chef's done their order.' She nodded towards the conference room.

Leanne didn't sound like her usual bubbly self and Elena noticed. 'That's fine and you're right, Leanne, see to the guests first, thanks. Are you okay? You don't seem your usual self this afternoon?'

'It's the thought of serving that man after hearing some of your conversation,' Leanne lied. 'He gives me the creeps.'

'Of course. Leave it with me and I'll get someone else to do it. But there's no way he would try it on with anyone while Mike's in there with him. It was unfortunate that he stepped out of the room while I was in there. Are you sure that's all it is?'

'Isn't that enough?' Leanne asked.

Elena decided to leave it. 'Go and order their teas, please, Leanne, and then sort this mess out. I'll organise the rest.'

'Thanks, Elena,' Leanne said.

As Elena watched her hurry towards the kitchen, she determined to discover what was really wrong with Leanne before she finished work that evening. Then she smiled to herself. Matt was in the sky, en route to her. Elena planned to make it a night he'd never forget and for him to have the holiday of a lifetime. Her good mood restored, she went to find one of her assistants to organise the kitchen so that Leanne didn't have to come into contact with the heinous Rob Green.

Chapter 4

'Ladies and gentlemen, we have begun our descent into Vouni. Please turn off all portable devices…'

Bob and Keith opened their eyes as the cabin crew boss made her announcement, and both stretched. They'd obviously had a good sleep and Matt was envious. Soon they were all looking out of the window as the aircraft made a steady descent towards its destination.

They'd dipped under the few clouds; the sky was now clear and the landscape was coming into view; craggy mountains with the sea off into the distance.

'Look at that,' Bob said, pointing from his window seat.

Matt and Keith leaned over towards the window to get a better look and saw a sea of pale pink in the distance.

'Flamingos,' Matt said. 'They're here for the rainy season before moving on.'

'Rainy season? You didn't tell us that, Matt. And what if one of those birds decides to fly into our path at the same time as the plane's landing? I don't want to be a statistic on *Air Crash Investigation*!'

'Typical you, Bob, always looking on the bright side,' Keith said. Both he and Matt laughed, but Bob remained stony-faced.

'They call it the rainy season but there's still plenty of sunshine and if Souvia does have a bad winter, it doesn't usually start until January. As for the flamingos, there's no record of them causing a plane to crash, though there have been a few rare incidents of birds dying at the airport—but they're few and far between.'

Bob seemed to be satisfied with the answer but his mates were used to him seeing a glass half empty, so weren't concerned. 'How far to the hotel?' he asked.

'About a thirty-minute drive. Plenty of time to settle in and have a look around before dinner.'

'And when do we get to meet your secret girlfriend?' Bob asked.

'This evening–and Elena isn't a secret. We wanted to get to know each other before telling friends and family is all.'

Bob nudged Keith knowingly and Matt shook his head, feigning annoyance at the immaturity of his mates. The conversation stopped as the plane landed and the passengers started fidgeting, checking their phones, impatient to unbuckle their seatbelts and to get out into the fresh air. Outside, they stopped to admire the cloudless blue sky and the sun that was heading towards the west. It was early afternoon and pleasantly warm.

'Rainy season, eh?' Bob said, as they made their way to the shuttle bus that was to take them to the airport buildings.

Less than twenty minutes later, the men exited the airport and followed the signs for their pick-up. Elena's directions were spot on and Matt was the first to see the minibus with *Griffon's Rest* emblazoned on its side in black letters, the *O* filled by a bright yellow sun. Two couples also boarded the minibus.

There were the usual ooohs and aaahs that the driver was used to from tourists who were visiting his beautiful island for the first time. Traffic was busy at both the airport and on the highway, but Matt noticed it was a lot lighter as they exited the highway and continued their journey on the minor roads. The views were stunning and he looked at the sea in the distance and felt his whole body relax. That changed when they pulled up outside the Griffon's Rest hotel and he saw her standing outside the main door, waiting for the minibus. His heart rate quickened at the sight of Elena who he hadn't seen for almost two months. She was as lovely as he remembered. Bob nudged Keith as they followed Matt's eyes.

Matt was at the door before the minibus stopped and he jumped out as soon as he could. His usual reserved nature was forgotten as he lifted Elena off the hotel pavement, and swung her around, before kissing her passionately.

'Ahem,' Bob coughed.

Matt and Elena came up for air.

'I take it this is Elena?' Keith asked.

Matt remembered his manners and was about to make the introductions when the sound of raised voices caused them all to turn around. A stocky man with a generous paunch walked out of the hotel, shouting as he did so. 'You'd be nothing without my help. Call yourself a mate? You're a flaming scrounger, just like the–'

'Scrounger! You have the nerve to call me a scrounger when you're a thieving–' The man following the first appeared to take a deep breath to compose himself, then continued in a quieter voice. 'You're a money grabbing sod, Rob Green, and all you do is take advantage of people who are going through tough times. I should have listened to the warnings but I couldn't see it. I trusted you!' He gave a bitter laugh. '…and look where that's got me. You'll not get away with this. I'm going to stop you. Do you hear me? I'll do whatever it takes to stop you from ruining my business.'

'It's in the bloody contract!' Rob Green replied, shouting at the top of his voice.

By this time, the two were facing each other and Matt, Bob and Keith could see what was coming and rushed to intervene. As they reached the front door, the second man's face was a breath away from the one he'd called Rob. 'Whatever it takes,' he said, emphasising each word with a poke in the other man's chest.

It was too much for Rob to take and he drew back his fist and punched the other man in the face, sending him flying to the ground. He lifted a foot as if to give the man a kick but saw the tall, imposing figure of Keith looming over him.

'I think that's enough now,' Keith said.

The man looked like he was going to have a go at Keith until Elena joined them. 'I think you'd best leave, Rob,' she said, then turned her back to him as she bent down to help the man on the floor.

'Are you all right, Mike?'

'I will be,' he said. 'As soon as I get that scumbag out of my life once and for all.'

It looked to Matt like it was going to kick off again so he held out a hand to the man on the floor, which the man accepted, and Matt pulled him to his feet.

'Mike attacked me!' Rob said to Elena, 'yet you're acting like it's my fault.'

Elena forced a false smile. 'I'm just trying to separate you and Mike and trying to diffuse the situation, Rob,' she said as politely and calmly as she could. 'And also trying not to put on the wrong type of show for the guests.'

A small crowd had gathered inside the lobby and were openly watching the proceedings.

'Shall we get you cleaned up?' Matt asked the man, and Elena gave him a grateful look. When Mike nodded, the pair walked into the hotel and Matt followed him to the guest toilets on the ground floor.

It was well appointed and there were small individual towels for guests to use to dry their hands. Matt put some next to Mike as he washed his face.

'Thanks,' he said, dabbing at the blood below his nostrils. One eye was already swollen, along with his nose. His face looked a mess. He was either not in pain, or had decided to ignore it as he continued. 'I've known Rob for years and always known he's an astute businessman, but I never thought he'd screw me over like this.'

Matt gave an enquiring look.

'It's no secret that it's been a bad few years for those of us in the hospitality industry. The worst ever. I own a small chain of restaurants in the U.K. – you might have heard of Goodman's? Anyhow, Rob offered to give me a loan at a lower rate than my bank. Even knowing his reputation, I thought our friendship might mean something to him.'

'So, you weren't able to pay him back?'

'Oh, I had no problem paying him back but my accountant went on maternity leave and made a small error before she left, which was nothing to do with my company not having the money. We're gradually getting back on our feet now and our clients are loyal and love us, thankfully. But for that one small mistake, Rob, in his wisdom, has decided the penalty will be an extortionate amount of interest, and that's what we fell out over.'

'Is there a contract?'

'Yes, and I guess it's in the small print. But if the roles were reversed I wouldn't do what he's doing. Not when we've known each other for years and are, sorry, *were*, friends. Honestly, I'm bloody furious and if the man were to drop dead tomorrow, I wouldn't be more happy! Now you know. Thanks for your help, mate, I appreciate this isn't a good way to start your holiday.' He laughed, then winced at the pain. 'I think I need to get home and explain this to my wife before she hears it from somebody else. News travels fast on this island.'

'Perhaps you should see a doctor first and also consider reporting this to the police. You have been assaulted.'

'Nah, a bit of TLC from my wife will do the trick. And as for Rob Green, I'll deal with him my own way.' Mike said, before putting the used towels into the wash bin next to the sinks. 'See you.'

Matt watched as he left the bathroom, wondering exactly what *his own way,* was.

It wouldn't be long before he'd have his own opinion about that.

When Matt returned to Elena and his friends he was glad to see that Rob Green had already left. The group were talking, so he didn't need to do the introductions.

She smiled when she saw him. 'I'll get someone to show Keith and Bob to their rooms, Matt.' She said then turned to Matt's friends, 'I've booked a table for dinner for the two of you at 7pm; that'll give you plenty of time to settle in. I hope that's okay? You can always pop to the bar before dinner or explore the facilities. There's a shuttle bus into town every fifteen minutes. It takes less than ten minutes.'

'Seven o'clock is fine, thanks,' Keith said. 'We'll chill or explore a bit before that as the mood takes us. We'll see you in the morning, Matt, ready for a round of golf?'

'Yup. Ready to leave here at 8.30?'

'Great,' said Bob, then added, 'have a good night.' He winked and Elena rolled her eyes. Their carry-on suitcases had disappeared, so Matt guessed they'd been taken to their rooms while he'd been speaking to Mike, in the bathroom.

As Keith and Bob entered one lift with a member of staff, Elena took Matt's hand and they headed for another. They managed to keep their hands off each other as the lift took them to the penthouse suite, but as soon as the door closed behind them, their lips locked.

'My God, you're beautiful,' Matt said, losing himself in the delights of Elena's soft olive skin. She smelled like flowers and he'd come to recognise a hint of her favourite perfume, Chanel Number 5, as they rediscovered each other. They were both eager and desperate, and after the months apart, their lovemaking was urgent.

Panting, Elena lay on her back after it was over and turned her head to Matt who was leaning on one elbow, facing her. 'Did you miss me?'

'Like you'll never know. I love you Elena.'

'Really?'

Matt frowned, having hoped for a different response. 'I love you too.'

The frown turned into a smile. 'Really?' They both laughed and said, 'Yes really,' in unison, laughing again.

Out of nowhere, Matt grabbed Elena's waist and tickled her.

'Gerroff,' she said, as she got her own back, and within a few seconds they were both in fits of laughter. Previous thoughts of whether one would feel the same about the other disappeared along with the laughter as they explored each other's bodies again, this time without urgency.

It was almost 8 o'clock when Matt's stomach rumbled.

Elena disengaged her body from his reluctantly. 'I'll order room service,' she said, getting up and putting on a robe. 'Then we can talk about what we're going to do for the rest of the week when you're not with your friends.'

Matt raised an eyebrow suggestively and Elena chuckled. 'As well as this, you'll want to see some of the island, surely?'

'Whatever you say, my love.'

Happy in their love cocoon, they did little talking that night, neither knowing that their plans would be scuppered following a discovery the following day.

Chapter 5

Sasha knew Mike's meeting with Rob would be difficult and wanted him to relax so they could enjoy the weekend together. He'd been stressed out with money worries after the last year and they'd had to tighten their belt, but now things were on the up and he'd said earlier that he was planning on paying Rob's loan off in one. That was when he'd looked at the paperwork and discovered the last payment hadn't been made and was already two weeks late.

'He'll invoke the penalty clause,' Sasha told her husband after he'd been in touch with the accountant.

'I don't even know what that is.' Mike laughed. 'We're friends, love, there's no way Rob'll do that.'

She shook her head as she recalled looking at her husband and thinking that, for such an astute businessman, he could be quite naïve at times.

The mince had browned while she'd been daydreaming and Sasha took it out of the pan and put it to one side in a dish. She put the onions in the pan, and the carrots on to boil. Despite owning a chain of restaurants, Mike was a man of simple tastes and loved her mince and potatoes, or Glasgow caviar as one of his Scottish friends called it. Sasha didn't care what it was called. She could take it or leave it but as long as it made Mike happy, it was job done. As soon as the meal was cooked, she planned on going to the gym and getting rid of the bad mood caused by the revelations from Leanne.

Sasha's blood boiled as she remembered Leanne crying on the phone. The girl was prone to drama – she would have loved to tell her that she was talking nonsense, but it had a ring of truth and Sasha just knew that Leanne wasn't lying.

'Wait until I get my hands on that flaming woman, and our Stephen,' she muttered out loud, stirring the onions with the wooden spoon none too gently. She had to break this news to Mike who, if her assumptions were correct, wouldn't be in the best of moods anyway, when he came home. It was as if thinking about him had

32

conjured him up and, hearing the car come screaming up the drive, Sasha brought herself back to the present. Mike was much earlier than expected and she knew something was wrong, even before he stormed into the house. She took a few deep breaths to centre herself – the way her therapist had advised so that she didn't lose her temper – though she had ignored this advice earlier when she'd finished on the phone with Leanne and had already ordered the two replacement Lladro ornaments she'd smashed during her hissy fit.

Trying to look as domesticated as possible, Sasha fluffed up her hair, retied her apron and plastered a smile on her face before turning to her husband. Her smile disappeared instantly.

'He hit you?' Sasha was incredulous, then she felt her blood boil for the second time that day. 'He actually hit you?'

It looked sore and she knew she should take Mike to the medical centre to check whether his nose was broken, but she had to sort those Greens out, once and for all.

Sasha grabbed her car keys off the hook and pulled her apron off as quickly as she could.

Mike nodded. 'What are you doing, love? Where are you going?'

'That's the second time today those Greens have messed with my family and I'm not bloody having it! I'm going to sort both of them out, once and for all.'

She stormed out of the kitchen, slamming the door behind her, and leaving Mike to turn off the hob – the last thing he wanted was a house fire, on top of everything else. It wasn't until later that it occurred to him he should have wondered what else the Greens had done to cause his wife to flip her lid.

Chapter 6

Rob jumped into his Range Rover and drove the short distance to the Marlborough Hotel and Golf Resort. *His* golf course and resort, he reminded himself proudly. If it wasn't for his hard work and the fact that he'd diversified, his father's fortune would have been lost – he was absolutely certain of that. And Mike could be an idiot at times, unable to separate his personal life from business. He'd warned him about that before but now he realised it had fallen on deaf ears.

Now look what's happened, Rob thought as he arrived at the resort's main gates. The camera's scanner had already recognised the vehicle registration number and the big gates opened as Rob approached. Unlike the CCTV, when it was working, the scanner wasn't set to keep a daily record of the comings and goings of vehicles.

The security guard came outside to greet him. 'Evening, Mr Green. Nice to see you, Sir.'

That's what my hard work's got me; people respect me and call me Sir. 'Hello there,' Rob answered. 'Busy day?'

'Yes, Mr Green, it certainly has been. Busloads of people, some staying at the hotel and others with day or week passes for the course. And it's not even our busiest season.'

'Great, that's what I like to hear,' he replied, winding his window up to signal the conversation was over.

The man smiled, turned, and went back inside his security box. Luckily for him, Rob Green didn't see the face he made as he did so.

Whenever he had problems with people or issues to sort, his favourite place to do so was the golf course. Not a lover of nature per se, walking around the course, whether he was playing or not, always made things better and often enabled him to come up with creative solutions to problems that had been bugging him. It also calmed him when he was in a foul mood and always made him feel better.

Rob knew he didn't have much time. When the sun started to go down on the island, it set quickly, and as he walked from the first to the second hole, he saw the last players leaving the course in the distance and making their way to the club house. He decided he'd pop in later for a quick one before going home and instead of giving them warning, he'd take them by surprise. *It doesn't hurt to keep the staff on their toes and to show them who's boss*, Rob thought, and pulled himself up to his full five foot eleven inches as he did so. By the time he'd got halfway around the third hole, the sun had completely disappeared over the horizon and he switched on the torch he'd brought with him. Thinking about Mike, he acknowledged that friendship was now down the pan. He didn't think Mike would report the incident to the police but there was a possibility that he would sue him for assault. Which meant the penalty clause money he'd receive for the late payment could well go back to Mike in some sort of compensation or, knowing Mike, as payment for medical treatment. Instead of being annoyed now, Rob shook his head and smiled to himself. Whatever happened, everything in life was all about money.

Not everyone in Rob's sphere of influence agreed.

Feeling a little breathless towards the end of the third, Rob slowed his pace. As he approached the green at the fifth, it was now pitch black. For some reason his vision was blurry; Rob wondered if it was anything to do with the darkness and reminded himself to book that eye test he had put off for months. He had been feeling better for the walk but as he continued along the downward slope, his breathlessness worsened. He shook his head, deciding to work on his fitness as he was beginning to feel like an old man.

Not feeling well at all, Rob decided to turn left, out into the open and past the green, instead of going to the right. Time to call it a night. He also decided to head home straightaway and not to call in to the clubhouse. He had an unusual desire to see Fiona and wanted to spend as much of the night with her as he could, if she didn't have other plans. Along with his blurred vision and breathlessness, Rob was now starting to sweat. He wanted to get back to his car and walked as fast as his body would allow.

Rob's phone vibrated in his pocket. He'd put it on silent as he always did when on the golf course. Trying to clear his head, he decided to take the call. He looked at the screen. Caller Unknown was on the display. He touched the red button and refused the call. Seconds later the phone went again, and for a second time, Rob declined it. By the fourth time, he was struggling to breathe and decided to answer the call to ask the caller to get help.

'You're getting it,' the voice said.

'Who is this?' Rob asked, in between trying to catch his breath. When he'd finally managed to say, 'Hello? Hello?' the call had already been terminated and Rob put his phone back in his pocket. He only wondered who it had been for a few seconds, his main concern now was to get some help for whatever was causing his breathing problems and the blurred vision.

Rob stopped and took a deep breath. He felt better for a second and when he had a chance to think about something other than his breathing, somewhere in the dark recesses of his mind he knew he had recognised the voice on the phone, but couldn't yet recall who it belonged to. He didn't have time to think about it further as he heard a thud to his left. Rob shone his torch towards the noise and saw that a golf ball was bouncing a few yards away from him. He heard the same words again, 'You're getting it,' but this time, it was in low tones and sounded tinny, as if being muttered through an amplifier. Rob didn't have time to think about the voice as a spotlight flared, blinding him, and golf balls began to rain through the air. He quickly realised they were being aimed directly at him.

'Not so clever now, are we?' the voice said, followed by laughter.

'You'll pay for this,' Rob shouted, between struggled breaths. 'I'll throttle you as soon as I find out who you are.' Then he shouted as a ball hit him on the thigh. Knowing he was exposed, Rob shone the torch in front of him, wondering why the light was blurred. He tried to run but the breathlessness kicked in again and this time it was worse. As quickly as he was able, he headed for the cover of the bushes in the distance. His thoughts formed slowly as he tried to work out how long it would take him to find cover. He was struggling now and fighting as hard as he could to get oxygen into his lungs. His brisk walk had turned into a struggle to stay upright and from a distance he looked like a drunk, swaying from side to side, while also trying his best to avoid the balls being fired at him.

The balls continued to follow him, most of them missing their target, the shooter believing that Rob's staggering and swaying was his way of trying to avoid them.

The voice still taunted him as he tried to up his pace. As his anger increased so did his heart rate, and he was determined he would make the individual pay, whoever he was, if it was the last thing he ever did.

The bushes were all but a touch away and Rob was about to take cover when he felt a sharp pain in his chest, and then his left arm. A nano-second later, a ball hit him on the side of his head. He went down like a bag of spuds.

'No!' the shooter said a few seconds later, watching in horror through his binoculars as his victim stayed on the ground. He turned the machine off and waited for Rob Green to get up and walk away, hoping his prank had taught the man a lesson. 'Come on, come on,' he said to himself, but there was no movement after a few minutes. He picked up the ball delivery machine, and the rest of his bits and pieces, and hurried back towards the car park. Then he looked at the machine under his arm and changed his mind. He returned to his car empty handed and left the resort shortly after, heading for The Griffin's Rest in time to start the night shift.

When Sasha arrived at Fiona's, the house was in darkness. She banged on the door anyway but resigned herself to the fact that her so-called friend wasn't in and knew she'd have to wait until the following day to have it out with her. Walking back to her car, she kicked a plant-pot in frustration.

'Arrggh,' she screamed, as the pain throbbed through her foot and up her leg, and she hobbled back to the car, cursing Fiona under her breath as she did so. She rubbed her foot when she was back in her car, and waited for a few minutes until she felt the rage subside. Then she sent a text. *You'll be sorry. I'll make you pay for what you've done!*

Sasha had no idea how she'd make her ex-friend pay – she couldn't shame her on social media without embarrassing her own family and Leanne and there was no way she was going to do that. The important things in Fiona's life were money, reputation, having fun, and her husband, probably in that order, so she would need to get at her in one of those ways. The throbbing in her foot had now stopped so Sasha picked up the can of red spray paint that she'd bought on the way from a DIY shop on the way. She went back to the front door and the security lights came on again. Fiona would know it was her but she didn't care. And she didn't care that the CCTV camera was more than likely recording her movements as she sprayed the word, *Bitch!* on the door. She stepped back to admire her work, looked up to where she thought the camera might be, then stuck her middle finger in the air. Now feeling slightly better, Sasha returned to her car and drove off.

She re-thought her initial plan about confronting her son at work. As much as she was bloody furious with Stephen, she didn't want him to lose his job. If he did, it would also jeopardise his course, because the hotel was sponsoring his degree and intended to formalise his management appointment once completed. Despite being spoilt, he seemed to be resigned to his current situation, and she'd heard good reports from acquaintances who had stayed at the hotel. *At least he's doing something right,* she grudgingly thought.

By the time she arrived home, she'd calmed down and Mike was relieved.

'How are you?' she asked.

'I went to A and E,' Mike said. 'My cheekbone is fractured but it will heal itself. They've given me some painkillers and I'll arrange another appointment at Outpatients in a few weeks, just to make sure everything's okay. It's painful but I'm fine, love.'

'And the police?'

'Just leave it, Sasha. I'm not going to report it.'

'When you hear what I have to tell you, you might just change your mind,' she said, noticing that Mike hadn't finished the dinner preparations. Sasha went to the kitchen and put the partly cooked food in the bin. 'Shall I order a takeaway? Then I'll tell you why I was so mad earlier.'

When Sasha had finished telling Mike about Leanne and Stephen splitting up, Mike changed his mind about reporting the incident to the police. 'It might be the only way to get back at that poisonous couple,' he said in disgust. 'I have plenty of witnesses. Take some photos of my face, love, before the swelling goes down too much, and the police can use this as evidence. As much as I'm not in the mood for going anywhere tonight, I'd better not delay it until the morning or they'll think I'm not that hurt or bothered.'

'Good idea,' Sasha said, already putting her shoes on to go out. 'And Stephen?'

'He needs to grow up and to realise he can't go through life acting like he does. I'll deal with him tomorrow but I've had enough, Sasha. I'm going to throw him out and make him stand on his own two feet. Are you with me on this?'

Sasha bit her bottom lip. Despite everything he'd done, he was still her baby, and her adored only child. Again, she acknowledged that she'd spoilt him and, although he'd gone off the rails a few years before, they had both thought that he had now grown up and was knuckling down. It appeared they were wrong.

'I'll support you, Mike,' she replied, 'but it's not going to be easy.'

'It won't be easy for me either, love, but if we don't do something now—' He left the rest unsaid and they closed the front door and headed to the police station to report the earlier assault.

Sasha wasn't the only one taking photographs. When the security lights came on after Fiona parked up, she saw the word scrawled over her front door.

'Damn her!' Fiona said out loud, and took out her phone. She photographed the image and pondered for a moment whether to report it to the police. Deciding against it in case Rob asked too many questions, she realised his car wasn't in the drive and wondered briefly where he was. He often had business meetings or short-notice problems to deal with but usually phoned to let her know he'd be late. Rob also knew that her relationship with Sasha could be volatile as they both had quick tempers, so Fiona hoped he'd assume that they'd fallen out over something trivial which caused her friend to vandalise the front door. It was a stretch, and given the choice, she would rather he didn't see it. She opened the door and went inside, keying the code into the security panel on the wall so the alarm wouldn't go off.

Fiona went to the kitchen and poured herself a glass of wine. Then she sat down and made the call to Dave the handyman, on the off chance that he might be able to come and remove the paint that night. It simply did not occur to Fiona to try to clean it herself.

Dave was at the other end of the island watching a football match, he told her when he returned her call an hour later, but would be there first thing in the morning. Not even the offer of extra money could entice him to come out that night, and Fiona thought he'd sounded tipsy. She popped the ready-prepared meal in the fridge into the microwave. Their housekeeper had made individual Shepherd's pies. After it pinged, she put the carrots and peas in and poured herself another glass of wine. She put the TV on for background noise and sat at the table to eat. She thought again about what to tell Rob regarding the door when he came home, and started to wonder what she could use as a believable reason for falling out with Sasha. She knew this was the death-knell for their friendship so it had to be a good one.

She would discover the following day that her musings had been in vain.

Chapter 7

The image of a teenage girl listening to her music via her headphones and reading her book popped into Matt's dream. It quickly turned to horror as the carriage flipped, and when it came to a standstill the former image was replaced with that of a mangled body with a missing arm, blood running down one side of her face and open brown eyes, staring in horror. He opened his eyes, forgetting where he was for a moment, and sat up in bed. Matt exhaled heavily then remembered exactly where he was and felt her eyes on him.

'Nightmare?' Elena asked.

'Yes,' Matt said, and gave his head a quick shake, as if to clear it of the dream.

'Like the one in England?'

'Yes,' he said again, before leaning over and kissing her on the cheek. 'The train crash again. I just have to live with it, but I'm okay. I'm going for a shower.'

Elena watched as he walked to the en suite bathroom and closed the door behind him, signalling the end of discussion on that topic. She put on her gown and switched on the kettle. By the time Matt had finished in the bathroom, his first coffee of the day was waiting and Elena went to get herself ready for a busy day at work in the hotel.

'Enjoy the golf. See you for dinner tonight,' she said shortly afterwards, about to head towards the door.

'Come here,' he said, pulling her back. The fearful expression that Matt had woken up with had long since disappeared. He put his arms around Elena and their lips met.

She came up for air after a long kiss. 'As much as I'd love to stay, I have work to do and you've arranged to meet your friends. I don't want to be the topic of conversation on the golf course.

He laughed and let go of her and Elena slapped his behind before leaving for work.

Feeling hungry, Matt decided to go to the restaurant for breakfast before he met his friends for a round of golf. They'd had the same idea and Matt saw them sitting at a table when he entered the room. He went to join them.

'Well, lookie here! Somebody's got a spring in his step and a smile on his face and it's nothing to do with being on holiday,' Keith said, grinning.

And that set the tone for the breakfast as they ribbed him gently. Matt knew they'd soon get fed up if he didn't bite, and as they finished eating, the topic turned to golf and who was likely to come second. Neither Matt nor Keith expected to beat Bob. When he was on form he was the undisputed best player of the three with a handicap of eight compared to Keith's of eighteen with Matt playing off a respectable fifteen.

They'd paid for extra luggage and brought their own clubs with them, and they'd also pre-booked their slots, so they were well organised by the time they arrived at the Marlborough Hotel and Golf Resort. They followed the signs to the reception, past the row of buggies in the outside area, and went to book in.

'Should we have booked buggies?' Bob asked.

'Strapping blokes like us?' Keith said, and the others laughed. 'Let's do today without buggies and see how we feel after we finish.'

'Sounds like a plan,' Matt said, his standard reply when agreeing to most comments.

'Tee-off time of 9.30, gentlemen?' the receptionist asked as they booked in and collected their score cards. 'You have time to use the Driving Range or you can go straight to the course.'

They decided to warm up for ten minutes on the driving range. The course master, who introduced himself as Christos, was waiting at the tee-box to the first hole. Without further ado they started their game.

By the time they got to the fifth hole they were lost in the game, and as expected, Bob had won holes one to four, and was on top form so far. Keith was second, with Matt having a nightmare game and bringing up the rear.

'I'm not going to make it so easy for you from here on in,' Keith said to Bob, 'just watch this space.' True to his word his drive was straight and true and the second shot took him in line with the green. Unfortunately for Keith, it all went wrong and the third shot took his ball into the bushes. The others were already on the green, and knowing there was a maximum time limit of three minutes to find the ball, it was all hands on deck as the search commenced.

'There's a lot of balls here,' Keith said. 'This seems a bit weird.' He pointed to an area and the others looked. 'There seems to be a trail of them heading this way,' Matt said, and started following the trail of balls.

He was the first to see a hand in a small gap between the bushes. He did a double-take and his eyes followed the hand up to a man's chest and then to his face, recognising it to be Rob Green, the man they'd witnessed assaulting his friend, Mike Goodman, shortly after their arrival the night before.

'Guys,' he called to the others and they hurried over, recognising something was wrong by the tone and urgency of Matt's voice. It took a moment for them to register what they were seeing, as it had with Matt.

'I guess that's put paid to this round of golf,' Bob said. 'Cheers Mr Green!'

'And there's me thinking our days of dealing with dead bodies were over,' Keith added.

Matt ignored them as he fished his phone out of his pocket and called the emergency services. Their years of training and experience on the job meant that they'd already carried out a quick assessment of the scene and of the body. A dark bruise had formed at the side of Rob Green's head, and considering the number of golf balls scattered around the area, it was obvious to all three that foul play had been involved That's what Matt told the operator.

'Someone is on their way now, sir,' the male voice on the phone said, and Matt was impressed that he had already despatched a vehicle while they were still talking. 'But what makes you think foul play is involved?'

Matt knew the call was probably being recorded – it was standard procedure in most countries – so he kept his comments succinct. 'A deep bruise on the deceased's temple, one that was likely made with a golf ball. Other balls scattered randomly around the area which the deceased could not have thrown himself. I'm former U.K. CID and so are the two friends I'm playing golf with.'

'I see. Please wait until the police and the medics arrive,' the voice said before terminating the call.

They waited as instructed, at a respectful distance from the body, and discussed what might have happened.

'Someone's taken shots at him from some type of ball-delivery machine, is my take on it,' Keith said.

'I agree,' Matt said, nodding, and Bob did the same.

The three men looked around, trying to assess where the perpetrator would have hidden.

'Hotel's too far away,' said Matt, looking towards the building in the distance. 'But he or she definitely knows this area well and must have known that the course dips down here. They could have chosen any number of spots to position themselves.' He turned in a circle, pointing as he did so.

'I would say over there,' Bob said. 'Just by the way he's lying, the killer ball most likely came from that direction.'

The men looked at each other and Matt and Keith nodded in agreement.

'I guess we should tell the course master,' Keith said, and volunteered to head back to reception to give them the gruesome news. He lolloped off at a jog, the others knowing that with his long legs and superior running ability, he would be the fastest. After running for a minute or so, Keith encountered one of the groundsmen and explained that they'd found a body. The man's face turned a sickly white colour almost immediately, and Keith prepared to catch him if he fainted. 'Are you–'

'Shocking,' the man answered, but seemed to compose himself as he took out his phone. He made a few calls, speaking in Greek. Satisfied now that he wasn't going to faint, Keith headed back to the others. Two buggies passed him on the way, heading in the same direction.

The course master kept his staff from gawking at Rob Green's body and got onto Reception, telling them to cancel all bookings for the rest of the day. They would lose money but knowing the Souvia police as he did, they'd have him down as a troublemaker if he didn't cooperate from the off, so better to be onside. And after all, respect had to be shown when the owner of the facility had died.

Four uniformed police officers arrived shortly after, driven on buggies by some of the course staff and they heard another siren in the distance. Matt and his friends watched as the medics arrived and eventually confirmed that Rob Green was definitely dead and not in a deep coma – something they all already knew but was a requirement to avoid the risk of a wrong decision being made. Seeing that they were still near to the scene, the police sergeant asked the three men to move to a distance away to wait.

'Somebody will be with you shortly, gentlemen, to take your statements. Please be patient and give us a few minutes.'

They did as they were asked and watched from a distance as the police confirmed that the course was to be closed, before cordoning off the area.

'Great start to our holiday,' Bob said, but the others ignored him.

As they watched and waited, Matt's mind was already going into overdrive as he wondered who could have killed Rob Green. Then he recalled Elena telling him that her father had talked her into taking a loan from Mr Green. He took his phone out of his pocket and flicked off the *silent mode* button so he would hear incoming calls. 'I'll be a few minutes,' he said to the others, walking away as he pressed the call button. The phone rang and rang and Matt was about to give up when she finally answered.

'I'm in a meeting,' she said.

'This is urgent,' Matt replied. 'I need to speak to you now.'

Hearing the seriousness in his voice, Elena said, 'Hang on.'

He heard her say, 'Sorry, I need to take this. Take a break and be back at eleven fifteen, please.'

After a pause where a door closed and there was no further background noise, she returned to the call, 'What's happened.'

'It's bad news, Elena, sorry. We've found a body on the golf course.'

'Oh my God! How awful for you. What happened? Are you all right? What about the others? Are they–?'

'Yes, we're all fine. The thing is, we know who it is.'

'You know him? I assume it's a man? How can you know him, you've only been here since last night?'

'It's Rob Green, Elena. We recognised him straight away.'

'Oh my God, Matt. My God!'

He gave her a second to take in the information, then she asked again what had happened.

'We found him and called the authorities–it looks like foul play was involved. They're securing the area at the moment and no doubt someone senior will arrive shortly to take a statement from us three. But in the meantime, I wanted to warn you. If their procedures are anything like ours they'll want to interview anyone who they consider to be suspects. That could include people who owe him money, Elena. So, I–'

'Foul play? You're saying I might be a suspect, or Dad? I can't believe this has happened here. And to someone I know. How awful.'

'I'm not saying you're a suspect, but they will probably want to eliminate you from their enquiries.'

'Ah, I see,' she said. 'Of course. You know I have nothing to hide, Matt. His poor wife. I've heard that she's not the most popular person but I wouldn't wish that on anyone.'

'It's a shock, Elena, and will be for everyone involved. If the police want to interview you let me know and I'll make sure I'm there to support you.'

'Oh, that's really kind, Matt, but I'm sure that won't be necessary. My cousin will probably interview me. He's just had a promotion and moved down this end of the island. I think he's quite high up in the police and with it being Rob Green, this will be quite high profile so George would want to be involved.'

'George?'

'Yes, he's a DCI now, I believe. I might give him a ring actually and see if he's heard.'

Matt paused for a moment to take in what Elena had just told him. Eventually he said, 'Your cousin is a DCI in the police and you didn't think to tell me?'

'Ah, well you're wrong there, Matt. So much for your detective work.' She laughed and Matt smiled to himself, glad that she could still do so despite what he'd just told her. 'I've arranged for us to have dinner with George and some other family members on my mother's side, later in the week. They're all dying to meet you, and I can't wait to show you off. George is working down this side of the island this week and I think he's going to move down here permanently, so it's all worked out quite well. I didn't have much of a chance to tell you last night, or this morning, as we were otherwise engaged,' she said, laughing again. 'I've got some other things lined up too. Can we talk about these tonight?'

'Of course, Elena,' he said, then noticed Keith beckoning him and pointing towards some other buggies that were arriving. Matt could see men in suits as the buggies drew nearer and rightly assumed the detectives had arrived. 'I have to go now, looks like the investigating officer is about to arrive.'

'Okay. Well if it *is* my cousin, tell him I said hello. See you later.'

'Will do.' Matt said, but Elena had already gone.

When he got back to the others, a man and a woman wearing suits were talking to the uniformed officers.

'How's Elena?' Keith asked.

'Shocked that we found a body, even more so that it's someone she knows. But she's okay. Her cousin is a DCI and she believes he might well be the investigating officer.

Bob raised an eyebrow. 'You didn't say.'

'There's still a lot that Elena and I don't know about each other,' Matt said. 'I'm meeting some of her family and having dinner with them later this week, when you guys will be freezing your butts off back in Blighty.'

Bob gave Keith a sceptical look which Matt caught.

'It's fine. Elena's not intentionally keeping anything from me. Trust me.' He was touched that they were trying to look out for him but also miffed that they were reading more into this than was there. He decided not to share Elena's business with them and had no intention of telling them about Elena's history with Rob Green.

The men waited on the grass near the bushes, away from the cordoned off area, as the police sergeant had asked them to do. Although early December, the sun was shining and Matt guessed it was approaching twenty degrees. They sat down on a patch of smooth grass and he closed his eyes and raised his head to the sun, letting it drain away any worries or concerns that he had. Matt guessed the others had done the same as none of them heard the man approach.

DCI George Constantinou studied the relaxed men for a moment, assuming from their demeanour that this wasn't the first dead body they'd encountered. 'Gentlemen,' he said, and all three opened their eyes, and then stood up.

'I'm DCI George Constantinou and I'm currently in charge of this situation until we discover what's happened. Thank you for waiting so patiently.'

Matt and the others introduced themselves one by one.

'Matt Elliott,' George repeated. 'Elena's partner? My cousin, Elena Lacey?'

Despite everything else that was going on, Matt's first thought was that he'd been referred to as Elena's partner and it gave him a sense of belonging, one that he hadn't had for a long time. It made him feel good. He brought himself out of his daydream, realising they were waiting for his response.

'That's right, George, good to meet you. I understand we're having dinner together later in the week?'

'Looking forward to that,' George said.

'Me too,' Matt replied.

Keith coughed gently and all eyes turned to him. 'We're all retired from the CID and are here to help if you need us,' he said.

'Thanks for the offer, but I'm sure we can manage.'

'I'm sorry, I didn't mean to suggest–'

George laughed. 'I'm sure you didn't. I trained both in the U.K. and here, on the island, and I worked with the Met for a while, so I'm used to dealing with murders, unfortunately. We'll wait for the post-mortem results but I'm pretty damn sure that this was a murder. Saying that, I believe that Mr Green was a U.K. citizen so we may have to involve some of your former colleagues. My team are already checking out his status. Now, if you wouldn't mind telling me how you found Mr Green, my DS will take notes as we go along.' When George finished talking he took off his jacket, and plonked himself down on the grass. 'Might as well be comfortable.'

The three men, and the DS, Chloe Petrou, joined him on the grass. It didn't take long and less than half an hour later they said their goodbyes.

'Do you fancy checking out another course? There's one near Vouni I'm told,' Bob said.

Keith looked at his watch. 'It's almost twelve now. I think we should leave it today and maybe explore the local area? I fancy a swim.'

'I'll leave you guys to it. I want to see how Elena's doing,' Matt said.

They made their way back to the hotel where Keith and Bob decided to go to the beach for a while before exploring some of the local area.

Elena had asked various members of her staff to keep an eye out for Matt, so as soon as the receptionist spotted the three men arriving, he made a call to his boss.

The three men arranged to meet later, and as Keith and Bob said goodbye to Matt, Elena appeared in the lobby.

'Can we talk?' she asked and Matt nodded. 'I'm not taking any calls,' she said to the receptionist as they made their way to the lift and to a room where they wouldn't be disturbed.

As soon as Matt closed the door behind them, Elena blurted. 'I need to tell you something.'

'What's wrong?'

'He made a pass at me yesterday, before you arrived, and before he fell out with Mike Goodman. I was going to tell you but knew you'd be annoyed and didn't want it to spoil our first night, so I thought it would keep until we met for dinner tonight.'

'Are you okay? Did he–?'

'I'm fine, Matt. I was annoyed and disgusted. I mean, suggesting that I would sleep with him for the loan to be paid off sooner. What sort of woman does, sorry, *did* he think I am!'

'A very attractive one, Elena, obviously, but totally out of his league.'

'Does this make me a suspect?'

'Well ordinarily it would.'

'But I have a rock-solid alibi,' she said, giving Matt a big smile, 'in the name of a good-looking bloke called Matt Elliott.'

'Exactly,' he said. 'And even if you didn't, I know you're incapable of such behaviour. I mean, firing golf balls at a person from a distance tells me somebody wanted to inflict pain, put the victim in a vulnerable situation, and enjoy watching. The perpetrator wouldn't necessarily have wanted to kill Mr Green, but that's a chance that he or she took. From the little I know about Rob Green, he sounds like the sort of man who would have lots of enemies.'

'You're right there, Matt. And after last night, Mike Goodman is at the top of my list.'

'Hmm. May seem a bit too obvious, and despite what he said to me when he was cleaning his face in the bathroom, I'm not sure he's the type of bloke who would hide. That's a bit cowardly—and my hunch is that if Mike Goodman wanted to inflict pain on Rob Green, he'd make damn sure that Mr Green knew about it.'

'Perhaps you're right. We'll wait and see what George has to say. I asked him to come over but, apparently he can't interview me because of the family connection, so someone else has to do it.'

'That makes sense, Elena. I'll be with you though, and I'll help you through it.'

'Don't take this the wrong way, Matt,' she said, laughing, 'but I'm quite capable of answering questions all by myself.'

'It can be a bit daunting and—'

'I've got nothing to hide, Matt, and I'm only telling the truth. How difficult can that be?'

It was a fair point and he agreed. He also gave himself a reminder that she was an independent woman and there was a fine line between being protective and overpowering.

'Well, in that case I'm off to the beach with the guys and you can tell me all about it when we meet for dinner.'

'Sounds like a plan, Matt,' she said with a smile, mimicking him, before giving him a quick peck on the lips. 'See you later.'

Chapter 8

DCI George Constantinou was indeed busy elsewhere. While the post-mortem was being arranged, George knew it was imperative for Mrs Green to be informed and he made his way to the Green's villa. DS Petrou was with him and he'd also brought along a female uniformed PC who could deal with most of the emotional fallout when they informed Mrs Green about her husband. They would leave PC Ionnou with the widow if necessary, if she needed someone to stay with her while she processed the shock of the news. It was a part of the job he hated. He looked out of the window – anyone who felt anything for other human beings hated this part of the job, he reminded himself.

The women were sitting in the front of the car, both quiet and contemplating the job no doubt, he thought. But for different reasons. Like him, DS Petrou would wonder if the wife had anything to do with her husband's death and surreptitiously look for any clues in her reaction, while PC Ionnou would simply want to comfort the woman and do anything she could to help her.

He leant forward in his seat. 'How are you feeling?' he asked PC Ionnou.

'I hate this part of the job, Sir, but so does everyone. It's not the first time and I'm focussing on getting it right, whatever the widow's reaction. It's important as this is one of the events that'll stick in her mind for years to come.'

'You're right. Nasty business and this is the worst part of the job. You never know how the bereaved are going to react to the shock.'

PC Ionnou gave a brief weak smile as she checked the traffic in her rear view mirror and indicated to exit the highway.

'What's your take on this, boss?' his DS asked.

'Looks like someone wanted to frighten Mr Green and it went horribly wrong. But you know, in our job, things are often not what they seem.'

'My thoughts too,' she said, and they carried on in silence.

'Wow!' PC Ionnou said some ten minutes later as they were about to start the ascent up the hill heading towards Orchard Heights, the impressive villa at the top.

DS Petrou jumped out of the car at the gates and pressed the intercom, fully expecting a voice to ask who she was. Instead, the gates opened. She got back into the car and they drove up the long drive. A sporty looking Maserati was parked up outside the front of the house and a red flashy Mercedes was sat at the top of the drive. Next to that was a small white van bearing a set of ladders on the top.

'Real Housewives of Souva?' Chloe said to PC Ionnou who gave a weak chuckle.

George had no idea what the joke was.

They parked on the other side of the Mercedes and approached the house. A man was working on the front door, scrubbing away at the word *Bitch,* which had been painted on the door in large red letters. George looked at Chloe and she raised her eyebrows.

'What's happened here?' the DCI asked, showing his badge to the man. The others followed suit.

'I guess Mrs Green upset her mad friend,' he said. 'They're in there now, going at it hammer and tongs. As bad as each other by the sound of it. The housekeeper closed the door so I couldn't hear them, but it was too late by then. Mrs Green and her friend's son like each other a bit too much by the sound of it, if you know what I mean.' He gave a suggestive wink and smiled after he'd finished talking.

'I see,' George said. 'Do you mind?' He indicated with an arm that he wanted to get to the doorbell.

The man moved and put his brush back into the bucket. 'No probs, I'm going for a break anyway,' he said, pulling his phone out of his pocket as he walked towards the cars.

A South East Asian woman opened the door, dressed in a skirt and top with an apron over both. 'Can I help you?' she asked in English, her voice loud and heavily accented. From her accent George guessed she was from the Phillipines. He also guessed she was speaking loudly in order to drown out the shouting from inside the home – it wasn't working. They showed their badges again.

'We're here to see Mrs Green,' he said.

Before the housekeeper could reply, two women headed towards the door, side by side and shouting at each other.

'You're like a bitch on heat!' one of the women was screaming, 'Stephen and Leanne would have got married and look what you've done. And you're not even sorry. You wait until I tell your scumbag of a husband. Then we'll see how sorry you are.'

'That's not going to happen, Sasha. I'm worried about Rob, he stayed out all night and it's so unusual for him—he always comes home, never mind how bad a day he's had.'

'Don't you talk to me about bad days. Your good-for-nothing sleazeball husband almost broke Mike's nose yesterday and that was after I discovered your latest bloody toy boy is my son! You're toxic, Fiona and so is that sleazeball husband of yours and we're finished, but not before I see you pay for this. Big style!'

The woman stormed past the visitors, her high heels clomping on the tiled floor.

'I can't help it if men adore me!' Fiona shouted back, 'And you'll pay for the criminal damage you've done to my home. I haven't finished with you yet either.' But her words fell on deaf ears as they heard a car door slam, followed by the sound of it speeding away, shortly after.

For the first time, Fiona realised she had visitors and George noticed Mrs Green clenching and unclenching her fists a few times, in an attempt to control herself, he thought.

'Mrs Green?' he asked.

'Of course. And what the hell do you want?' she asked–and then the PC's police uniform registered, and she took a step back. 'Sorry. I'm not having a good day so far.'

They showed their IDs and George made the introductions.

'It's Rob, isn't it? What's happened?'

'Can we go inside and talk please, Mrs Green?'

Fiona hurried through one of the doors leading off the extensive reception area and they all followed. 'Please, sit down,' she said, sounding like a completely different woman to the one who had just had a slanging match with her former friend. 'Is Rob all right?'

'I'm really sorry, Mrs Green, but it's bad news. I'm afraid that your husband's body was found on the Marlborough golf course at Griffon's Rest this morning.'

'No!' she shouted and a hand flew to her mouth, then she looked at each of them in turn. 'It can't be Rob!'

PC Ionnou moved to sit next to Mrs Green but the new widow shuffled to the side of the settee, putting some space between them.

'We're so sorry for your loss, Mrs Green,' the PC said, but Fiona ignored her and put her head in her hands. She started crying, then the silent tears turned to sobs and she started wailing and rocking herself forwards and backwards. PC Ionnou put her arms around Mrs Green and held her. George and Chloe got up from their seats and left the room. Chloe explained the situation to the housekeeper who had come running to the sound of her employer's grief. 'Bring some hot, sweet tea please,' she said and the woman hurried off to do as she'd been asked.

They returned to the room when they heard the sobbing had subsided.

'What happens now?' Fiona asked, peering up at George from swollen eyes.

'I know this has been a tremendous shock but we need you to come and identify your husband, Mrs Green.' George said. 'We'll also need to ask you a few questions but we can come back another time if you need some time on your own or with family or friends. We know it's a shock and–'

'No. Let's just get on with it. What happened to Rob?'

George got up from the chair and nodded towards PC Ionnou who moved so that he could sit next to Fiona. 'Unfortunately, Mrs Green, it looks like a number of golf balls were fired at your husband while he was walking around the golf course. We think this happened some time last night but are not sure yet. One of the balls appears to have hit him on the side of the head.' George touched his temple to show her where, then continued, '…and we think this may be what killed him. There'll be a post-mortem to confirm the exact cause of death.'

'So–Rob was murdered?' Fiona asked, folding her arms around herself as if in protection.

'We believe so, Mrs Green. Do you know anyone who might have had a grudge against your husband?'

'Huh!' she said, then gave a bitter laugh. 'How long have you got?'

'Are you sure you want to talk about this now, Mrs Green?'

'Like I said, let's just get on with it. I don't know much about the business but do know that a number of people owe us money, so you may want to start there. Mark Fletcher works exclusively for Rob for both the business and our personal finance. I'll give you his details.'

'The woman you were arguing with when we arrived…?'

'Sasha Goodman. We used to be best friends but our relationship has been toxic for a while and we're always falling out. Their business was in trouble and Rob helped them out–and look at the thanks we get!'

'Thanks, Mrs Green.' George paused, then added, 'It didn't sound like you were arguing about money when we arrived.'

Fiona started sobbing again. 'I think you're right. I don't want to do this now,' she managed, and then put her head down, struggling to control the sobs that were trying to spill out. When she lifted her head she looked distraught, wringing her hands and doing her best to hold it together. She shuddered and PC Ionnou put a gentle arm around her again.

Fiona shook it off. 'I'm fine,' she said and then addressed George. 'I need to see Rob to make sure it is him and to say goodbye.'

'Of course,' George said, nodding to Chloe who left the room.

She returned shortly after. 'A car's on its way, Mrs Green. It should be here in twenty minutes. PC Ionnou will accompany you there and back.'

'We'll arrange another time to talk to you, Mrs Green, when you feel better able to give us the information we need,' George said.

They said their goodbyes and George and Chloe left, leaving the PC to look after the widow for the time being.

'Mrs Green was having an affair with her best friend's son.' Chloe said, stating the obvious on the way back.

'Looks that way. So much for best friends, eh? We need to speak to him. In fact, we need to speak to Mr and Mrs Goodman as well as their son. That's next on the list, but first I need a list of the comings and goings at the resort so we can see if any one of them were on site when this happened. As it's gated, they've probably got CCTV, so get that checked. I also need Elena to be interviewed and eliminated from our enquiries.'

'Boss?'

'She told me they took out a business loan from Rob Green, so that also puts her on the list.'

'Right. I'll do that.'

'No, Chloe, you're too close too. Rob Green was a British Citizen so it's likely the U.K. will send someone over to join our investigation. I don't want them thinking this is Hicksville and that we're nepotistic. We are going to be whiter than white–although there's nothing stopping you from talking to your friends off duty, and if they disclose information without you probing for it, who are we to argue?'

'Got it,' Chloe said.

Back at the hotel, Elena was trying to get her staff back into the day-to-day routine, knowing that everyone was talking about the demise of the heinous Rob Green and speculating about how it had happened. Despite this, she noticed that something wasn't quite right between Stephen Goodman and Leanne Carter. Their body language gave most of this away, but she also felt there was something more going on than just Rob's death. Elena couldn't quite put her finger on it, so called Stephen and Leanne away from the other staff.

'Everything all right?'

'Fine,' Leanne said, though it obviously wasn't.

Stephen nodded, while chewing a nail.

'Clearly it isn't. I don't know what's going on with you two,' Elena said, 'but try to keep your personal lives out of the hotel. I don't want the clients to see surly or unhappy members of staff.'

'You might as well know, Elena. He cheated on me and we're no longer an item.'

'It wasn't cheating–I met someone else. We can't help who we fall in love with, Leanne, and I'm sorry. I didn't mean to hurt you.'

'Can't help who we fall in love with!' Leanne said, raising her voice. 'She must be at least twenty years older than you, maybe even more. A proper cougar – and now she's a widow you won't have to–'

'Enough!' Elena said.

Their shouting stopped immediately but the guests who had been watching continued to do so. 'I take it you're talking about Rob Green's wife?'

'That's exactly who I'm talking about. And probably the reason his parents kicked him out and why he's living in one of the rooms in the hotel,' Leanne said, and gave a satisfied smile at the look of surprise on Elena's face. 'And

59

I wouldn't be surprised if he actually killed Rob Green, too, then they could just swan off somewhere and Stephen could be a kept man.' Leanne finished and folded her arms.

'Stephen?'

'That's preposterous,' he said, though his face had turned a funny shade of white. 'You know the saying about hell hath no fury like a woman scorned? Leanne just wants to get back at me because I don't love her any more. I wouldn't dream of trying to kill anyone, not in a million years.'

'I know that.' Elena frowned. 'I was actually thinking about… In fact, come with me to my office, now.'

Elena started walking and Stephen followed. 'You too, Leanne.'

'But I haven't done anything wrong.'

'I'll be the judge of that. Follow me, please.'

They were silent until arriving at Elena's office. She sat down and the others followed suit.

'Judging by Stephen's reaction, Elena, I think he is the one who did it. I'm not trying to say he purposely tried to murder Mr Green, but…'

'Are you Miss Marple all of a sudden?' Stephen interrupted.

'Stephen?' Elena asked.

'Of course I didn't do it,' he said.

'Well, they have CCTV of the people coming and going from the resort so at least they'll be able to check that and know who was about at that time. I heard they found him on the fifth or sixth hole, so by the time he left here and walked to that hole it would have been dark.'

'And?'

'And, Stephen, there wouldn't be any players on the course. Maybe one or two groundsmen, along with Rob Green, but that's about it,' Elena said. Seeing Stephen looking baffled, she continued, 'The CCTV at the gate will show the cars that left the resort last night after it was dark and I'm sure the police will round them up and question the registered owners. They'll get a guest list from the hotel so will know who had a genuine reason to be there, and who was up to no good.'

'I'm sure they would if the CCTV was working,' Stephen replied. A bit too smugly, Elena thought. 'But it's not. One of my mates works there and told me it's been broken for a while.'

'My cousin is in charge of the investigation,' Elena said, 'and he told me the CCTV was fixed earlier this week so it shouldn't take long to check the details.' She smiled. George hadn't told her any such thing but the colour drained from Stephen's face and he chewed a nail before dropping his hand back to his side. Elena knew he was keeping something from her. Now she wondered if he did have anything to hide.

'Are you all right, Stephen?'

'I've got to go.'

'What do you mean you've got to go? You're in the middle of your shift, you can't just–'

But it was too late–he was already heading for the door.

Elena looked at Leanne, expecting to see her looking worried or concerned at the very least. She was met with an expression of smug satisfaction. 'I need to make some calls,' Elena said. 'Get back to work and please, don't mention this to anyone just yet.'

'But–'

'No buts, Leanne. The police will deal with this and it'll soon be public knowledge, then you can talk about it all you like.'

Leanne walked off in a strop and Elena watched her for a second, recalling Stephen's words about a woman scorned. The love she'd clearly felt for him had apparently turned to hate in the blink of an eye. Not for the first time that day, Elena wondered if her assessment of Leanne and her suitability for employment had been totally off the mark. Sighing, she took her phone out of her pocket. The sooner she phoned the police, the better chance they'd have of catching Stephen, who Elena was convinced had something major to hide, even if he wasn't the one who had murdered Rob Green.

'George, I think Stephen Goodman might know something about who killed Rob Green, and I might have told a little porky about the CCTV at the resort.'

'I'm listening,' George said.

Elena quickly explained what had happened.

Three hours after Fiona Green had returned from the gruesome task of identifying her husband's body, Stephen Goodman, her ex-plaything, was apprehended at Souva Airport while attempting to board a plane destined for London. DS Chloe Petrou cuffed him, and with the help of a uniformed PC, put him in the car and drove him to the capital's Police Station, where transfer to Vouni Police Station was arranged shortly thereafter.

George and Chloe sat opposite Stephen Goodman in the interview room, and a uniformed constable was standing by the door. George nodded to Chloe who pressed the record button on the machine.

'Let's talk about the CCTV at the entrance to the Marlborough Hotel and Golf Resort,' George said, choosing his words carefully. If Stephen had bothered to contact his friend at the resort after speaking to Elena, he would have known that the CCTV system was still not working. But he had panicked and run. So although they didn't have any proof, George believed that Stephen's actions were those of a guilty man and now he just had to prove it.

It was a lot easier than he'd expected.

'I didn't mean to kill him,' Stephen replied. 'I was jealous that he was married to Fiona and I wasn't and I wanted to make him suffer.'

'Tell us how you went about that, Stephen.' George said, hiding his surprise at Stephen's words.

Twenty minutes later, they had a full confession and Stephen was taken to a cell. The post-mortem was arranged for Monday and DCI George Constantinou fully expected to be able to charge Stephen Goodman with murder, or manslaughter, at the very least.

Chapter 9

Elena had lots to tell Matt that evening at dinner and he was surprised at the pace the case had developed while he had been playing tourist along with Keith and Bob. He was even more surprised when his phone rang and the caller ID showed it was his ex-boss, Chief Superintendent Dale Rosewell.

'This could be important, Elena, sorry,' he said as he left the table to take the call.

Elena stopped eating and looked at Matt, wondering what could be so important it should interrupt his holiday.

Matt asked the same question.

'It's about the late Rob Green, Matt,' Dale said. 'He was a Brit so we would normally send someone to be part of the team.'

'I see. It seems quite a straightforward case and if Monday's post-mortem confirms cause of death as we all suspect, they're likely to charge the man they already have in custody.'

'I'm aware of that, Matt, but I'd like to hire your services for this one as you're already there. What do you say?'

'If you'd asked me earlier, Dale, I would have said that I'm very close to a possible suspect.'

'That'll be Elena Lacey I take it?'

'My! News does travel fast,' Matt said, frowning.

'I'm a copper, Matt, and a friend. Like your other friends, we haven't seen you happy for a while, so now that you are, some of your friends wanted to spread the good news. Anyway, what do you think about the job?'

Matt couldn't be annoyed, knowing people only had his best interests at heart. He also knew that most coppers liked to gossip with the best of them, but was still a little surprised that he was the subject of this gossip having left the force over a year before.

'Are you still there, Matt?'

'Yes I'm still here, and yes, I'm interested.'

'Good. I'll set it up. You'll need to re-attest so that you're back on the force. Is that okay?'

'Fine by me,' Matt said, 'As long as my work for you is on an ad hoc basis and not full time.'

'Definitely not full-time, Matt. Just as and when we need you. And of course, you can turn down any request as you see fit.'

'Sounds like a…sounds good to me,' he said, correcting himself halfway through his sentence.

'George Constantinou will be in touch in due course to go through the details with you.'

They finished the call and Matt returned to Elena. 'It seems I may be working with your cousin for a few days, at the very least.'

'Oooh. Do tell.'

'I'm being seconded to the Souvia Police as the British Police Representative to work on the case as Rob Green is a British Citizen. This sort of thing is common practice when a country's national dies abroad.'

'This might be the shortest secondment in history, bearing in mind they already have the chief suspect banged up,' Elena said with a twinkle in her eyes.

'We still have to wait for the post-mortem, Elena, and this all just seems too straightforward at the moment. My gut tells me that there's more to this than meets the eye.'

'I think you could be wrong, Matt.'

'Moi, wrong? Seriously, Elena.'

'It's just as well I hate false modesty. But we'll see, won't we?'

'We will indeed. Now shall we talk about something else?'

'Good idea, Matt. Let's talk about when you're going to come to live on my lovely island.'

The rest of the long weekend passed uneventfully, and on Sunday night, Matt had dinner with Keith and Bob before their departure the following day. They weren't leaving until Monday evening but Matt had received a text from

George telling him he'd pick him up at nine to take him to the mortuary where the post-mortem was to take place on Rob Green. He didn't expect to have the time to meet up with his mates again prior to their departure.

As Keith went to use the bathroom, Bob took the opportunity to have a quiet chat with Matt. 'We think she's good for you and she's a keeper, Matt. Are you going to move here?'

'That's the plan. I'm just not sure yet of the timings – and there's Jenny to consider.'

'Jenny?'

'The rescue dog I promised I wouldn't abandon. She's definitely coming with me wherever I go.' He didn't add that Jenny was the only one who kept him sane these days after the worst night horrors, and that she had chosen him as much as he had her.

'You'd risk all of this,' Bob swung his arm around in an arc, 'for the sake of a dog that you don't even own yet!'

'Not risk, Bob, it might take a little longer is all. And it's a case of love me…'

'…love my dog. You're a walking cliché, Matt. I don't believe this. Hey, Keith,' he said, as Keith approached the table, 'you'll never guess what Matt's just told me.'

'The dog.'

'You knew?'

'Yeah, and I get it. Don't knock it if it works and keeps you sane is what I say.'

'But it'll cost a fortune and I'm sure there's loads of dogs over here that need a home.'

'I'm sure there are,' Matt said. 'But they're not Jenny and they're not the one I've promised to look after.'

'You are bloody barking,' Bob said, shaking his head.

He wasn't an animal lover. Matt understood where he was coming from, but it didn't change anything. 'I've got a murder to investigate and you've got a game of golf to play so let's leave it at that. Enjoy, and have a safe flight. I'll give you a call when I get back and we can have a round in the miserable rain.'

'Looking forward to it already. Take it easy, Matt,' Keith said, putting his arms around Matt and slapping his back.

Bob got up and did the same, and after saying their goodbyes, Matt returned to the hotel room and waited for Elena to join him.

Chapter 10

Monday morning dawned bright and sunny, in total contrast to the gloomy task that lay ahead for the coroner's staff at the mortuary.

George was five minutes ahead of time but Matt was ready and waiting for the car to pick him up. DS Petrou drove while George and Matt sat in the back of the sturdy Mercedes police car.

'We have mortuaries at the main hospitals in our three cities,' George explained, 'and one is also attached to our forensic science laboratory about a fifteen minute drive from Vouni. That's where Mr Green is and that's where we're headed now. The Vouni Police Station is a few minutes drive from the mortuary. I've recently transferred there from Souva so that's the centre of operations for all of my investigations now.'

'Elena did mention you'd recently transferred and had a promotion.'

'It's not a promotion in rank, Matt, I've been a DCI for a number of years. But they've had a reorg and I'm now SIO for serious incidents in Souva so it's a promotion in that respect. My wife's family lives near Souva and Emily prefers this end of the island, and you know that saying about happy wife, happy life.'

'Indeed I do.' Matt said. He looked out of the window as they passed the signs for Vouni city centre. A few minutes later they came off the highway.

'What's your story, Matt? I know you run your own consultancy business now and you're seconded to us.'

'I'm a retired DCI,' Matt said, 'I had a full career with the police and left almost two years ago. Since then I've started my own business and most of the jobs I get are with my former employers.' He smiled. 'I guess they know I'm good value for money. But you probably knew all of this before recommending me for this role, George. Am I right?'

Now it was George's turn to laugh. 'You know how important gut instinct is in our line of work. Let's just leave it at that.'

Matt wasn't sure whether Elena's cousin really rated him or whether the family relationship had influenced his decision. It didn't matter to him as his record spoke for itself, and aside from the blip following the train crash, his achievements were obvious. This was an opportunity for a new start and he intended to be as diligent as he had been when investigating cases at the height of his career – his nature demanded it – he didn't have a choice.

They took a left and drove through the countryside for a few minutes. In stark contrast to the houses and business buildings visible from the highway, Matt now looked out of the window onto the beige landscape in the distance that was yet to be turned green by the winter rain. Chloe stopped the car for a boy to herd his goats across the road, and George smiled at Matt and shrugged his shoulders. Shortly after, she turned on the indicator and took another left turn. In front of them stood a rectangular white building which Matt guessed was about three storeys high.

'This is it,' DS Petrou said.

To the left of the large door was a silver placard with the words, *Souvia Forensic Services,* etched onto it. The door was locked. DS Petrou pressed the buzzer and looked straight at the camera.

'DS Petrou and…' she began but a voice interrupted her.

'Happy Monday!'

'It's Phil,' DS Petrou said, as they heard a click.

She pushed the door open and they entered the reception area.

'Just when you think the start of my working week can't get any better,' said the man on reception, 'but who should walk in but Chloe along with her wonderful DCI. And who do we have here?'

Dressed in his colourful clothes, and with his cheery attitude, the man looked out of place in the clear, stark surroundings. He reminded Matt of a peacock who preferred other peacocks to peahens.

'Matt Elliott. I'm seconded from the British Police because Mr Green is a U.K. National,' he said, holding out a hand which Phil took. Matt was pleasantly surprised at the firmness of the shake.

'Don't let all of this fool you, Matt,' Phil said, after they released hands. He wafted his hands around the front of his body, indicating his attire.

'I'll try not to,' Matt said, with a smile.

'Where's the boss,' George asked.

'Dr Kostas is in the lab now with the lovely Anna and they're dissecting the late Mr Green. He said to go to the gallery if you wish or to wait in the suite where I'll bring you refreshments and entertain you with my anecdotes if you'd prefer.'

George shook his head, trying to look irritated.

'The gallery it is then, I take it? If you'll just book in for me, you can then be on your way.' Phil pushed a book towards the visitors and they all signed in.

Although George and Chloe knew the way, Phil insisted on going with them, having changed the combination on the door the week before. They followed him along a short corridor, then up a set of stairs and along another corridor, and Phil finally stopped outside a door which had a small panel with numbers on. He keyed in the combination and turned the handle when he heard the click. 'See you all later,' he said, turning with a flourish and mincing back along the corridor.

It was a refreshing change to meet such a flamboyant character in such sombre surroundings, and Matt said so. 'He is entertaining but I think he should probably be on the stage and not in a mortuary,' Chloe said, as George led the way through the door and into the viewing gallery.

They leaned on the metal railings, watching the scene in the lab below. Matt was glad that they were unable to see what exactly was going on.

Having heard the door open, Doctor Kostas Demetriou and Doctor Anna Phillipou turned to see who had entered.

'Good morning, gentlemen; Chloe,' Kostas said, through the microphone that was attached to his face, as Anna nodded to acknowledge them.

'Good morning both,' George replied. 'Any news for us yet? Is it a case of accidental murder from the golf ball as we all suspected?'

'Indeed I have, and I'm afraid to say that no, it is not.'

The detectives looked at each other in surprise.

'I'll be finished in twenty minutes or so. Grab yourselves a coffee and I'll see you in my office.'

Monday morning was busier than usual for Elena. Stephen Goodman had been doing a stint as Assistant Manager in the Housekeeping Department and he had proved to be surprisingly diligent. She hadn't yet had time to recruit a replacement and Henry, the permanent Assistant Manager was away visiting his family and off for a week. Any queries came directly to Elena and she'd had to organise extra staff to clean a room where a guest had left a bath running after forgetting they'd turned it on and went out for an early morning walk. Some light bulbs needed changing, and she also had to speak to a guest about her allergy to the washing powder, and arrange to have towels washed separately in a different detergent to satisfy her needs. On top of this, Marina, the beautician in charge of the hotel's spa, now needed to speak to her *as a matter of urgency*.

Elena made her way to the basement where the indoor pool and spa was located. She peeped through the window, noticing two guests swimming in the pool, before making her way to the spa.

Marina's Sanctuary was as quiet as it usually was at this time on a Monday morning. Marina was behind a counter, rearranging a stack of white and turquoise towels that already looked immaculate to Elena.

'Good morning, Elena,' she said, when she became aware Elena arrived, but a frown creased her beautiful oval face and her brown eyes looked worried.

'Marina, what is it?'

'We've had a theft and I need to call the police.'

'A theft?' Elena's eyes did a quick inventory. She knew all the creams and treatment potions were kept in cupboards in the closed room behind the counter, and guests wouldn't necessarily know that room was there unless they saw Marina and her staff entering.

'What's missing?'

'Botox. I was off this weekend but we had a number of appointments on Friday. The fresh Botox arrived on Thursday and when I came in this morning, Celia told me she'd had to cancel Friday's appointments as the Botox wasn't there. As soon as she noticed, she contacted all of the clients, apologised and made new appointments. Our supplier is great, so they were able to deliver a fresh batch on Saturday for some of the rearranged appointments, and some of the other clients are coming today so we're fortunate that they were all so understanding.'

'But who would steal the Botox and why? They couldn't inject themselves, surely?'

'No, they couldn't, Elena. And, if they did try to inject themselves with that amount of Botox all at once, it would poison them. The amount we use on each client is tiny but what was stolen is enough to do some serious damage if it's used in the wrong way.'

'Seriously? I didn't know it was poisonous either,' Elena said, thinking for a moment. 'But why would someone want to steal it then? Do you think it's for another clinic or something?'

'What I think, Elena, is that whoever stole it is up to no good. I also think that they knew where to find it which makes me believe it's somebody who works here.'

'You can't go around accusing–'

'I'm not accusing anyone, Elena, just trying to think logically about this. There's something niggling at the back of my mind but it refuses to come out yet. I haven't got

72

any appointments until later today so I'll go for a run after I've reported the theft to the police. That may jog my memory.'

They both smiled at the play on words before Elena turned serious again. 'I hope it's nobody we know and that they don't work here. That would be awful.'

'I know. Let's hope I'm wrong,' Marina said, picking up her phone to call the police. Elena waited.

'They said they'd send someone but that it's not exactly a high priority. I'll get on with my work and if they turn up when I'm in an appointment, I'll just have to deal with it then.'

'Great. A fight in the hotel on Friday, a theft and a possible poisoner working for me. If we're not careful the Trip Advisor rating will go from five to one just like that,' Elena said, clicking her fingers.

'Yeah, let's just worry about our star rating, despite all the criminal activity going on around here,' Marina said, with a twinkle in her eyes.

'Okay, point taken, Marina. But if we don't have a good star rating we won't have bookings and some of the staff could lose their jobs.'

'Touche, Elena. If that's the case, then I hope the thief loses their job.'

'You're convinced it's one of the staff then?'

'I certainly am. When I get back from my run I'm going to make a list of everyone I remember coming in and out of the spa after the Botox was delivered and until it was discovered missing. Then we'll have more of an idea of who it might be.'

'Be careful, Marina, and don't get too carried away.'

'As if I would,' she said. 'I'll see you later.'

Elena noticed Marina lock the door to the storeroom before she left. As she made her way back to her own office, she certainly hoped that Marina was wrong but then a thought came to her; if Stephen Goodman hated Rob Green enough to kill him with a golf ball, might he have wanted to poison him first, just to make sure, or had he decided that the balls would be enough to do the job? Could he be their thief?

Doctor Kostas had showered and changed into a suit by the time he met the detectives in his office, some thirty minutes later. George gave him a questioning look.

'I'm in court this afternoon,' he said. 'The bullion robberies.'

George and Chloe nodded. Matt ignored his natural curiosity as he introduced himself, more interested about the pathologist's findings regarding the death of Mr Rob Green. 'I thought our conclusion about Mr Green's death might be too good to be true,' he said, following their handshakes.

'My verdict, gentlemen, and Chloe, is that Mr Green was poisoned.'

'Poisoned, Doc?' Chloe asked.

'Yup. Anna has a few more tests to run but it looks like the poisoning caused a premature heart attack at the time when your current suspect decided to fire balls at Mr Green.'

'You're saying that it wasn't being struck by the ball that killed him, but whatever poison was in his system?' George asked.

'Yes, that's exactly what I'm saying. The PM shows that the ball didn't hit him hard enough to do any serious damage. He would have suffered respiratory failure then died of a heart attack due to the Botulinum toxin in his system, even if he hadn't been attacked by golf balls. He might also have experienced blurring of vision and, most likely, confusion, prior to finally succumbing to the heart attack. But alas, we will never know.'

'Botulinum toxin?' Matt asked.

Dr Kostas nodded. His phone rang and he fished it out of his pocket. 'Anna,' he said, listening for a few seconds. 'Thank you, Anna. Okay, get cleaned up and write it up when we return from court.'

'Botulism spores can grow in food where it hasn't been heated enough to kill them, to at least eighty-five degrees centigrade to be precise; but this isn't due to anything that Mr Green ate voluntarily. We know that, not from the particles of undigested food in his stomach which were tested, but from the liquid that was in there. Anna took the samples and the tests confirmed it.'

'What do you think happened?' Matt asked.

'There were large amounts of the poison in the coffee Mr Green consumed only hours before his death. I take it that Mr Green didn't poison himself, so someone has done this on purpose. Normally Botulinum toxin is a slow acting killer but Mr Green may have also been allergic to the substance, causing a quicker reaction in his system. Discover where and when he drank coffee on the day he died, and you're on the right road to finding his killer.'

'We need to find out how the killer obtained the poison,' George said.

'Beauty salons maybe?' Chloe said.

Doctor Kostos smiled and the others looked at her. 'I believe that Botulinum Toxin can be found in Botox, widely used for cosmetic purposes and to treat conditions such as migraines, excessive sweating, and muscle spasms.'

'How do you know all of this, Chloe?' George asked.

'My Mum decided she wanted to slow the ageing process, though don't tell her I told you. I wanted to make sure it was safe and did a bit of research. She goes to Marina's Spa in Elena's hotel for her treatments every four months. It makes her happy and doesn't do any harm, so it's a win-win, situation.'

'Doc?' Matt asked.

'Chloe's spot on,' the doctor answered. 'There are no recorded incidents of Botox ever killing someone who's used it for cosmetic treatments, but qualified practitioners only use a tiny amount of it for these purposes. If the killer is a practitioner, he or she would have access to enough of the substance to cause the death of Mr Green. The substance is regulated so it should be relatively easy to discover who on the island has received it and delivery dates, etcetera, or, indeed, if there are any reported thefts of the substance. But bear in mind, there are also some people who do not follow the code of ethics for administering Botox and may obtain it through the black market. If that's the case, it won't be so easy to find.'

'Thanks, Kostas,' George said.

'Anything else?' Kostas asked.

'I think you've given us more than enough to work on. Please thank Anna for her diligence. We'll be in touch.'

They said their goodbyes and Matt drove back while Chloe spent her time Googling the clinics on island, then narrowing them down to those within the city region of Vouni.

Chapter 11

The niggle at the back of Marina's mind turned into a proper memory by the time she finished her run. Heading back to the hotel, she was convinced she knew who the thief was. As she rushed towards the main entrance, Marina didn't bother with her cool down exercises in her eagerness to tell Elena.

Elena was outside, talking to two guests.

'I've remembered!' Marina said, forgetting her manners.

'…and this is Marina who runs the sanctuary and spa in our basement,' Elena said to the older couple. 'Next to our indoor pool.'

The woman smiled at Marina. 'And what have you remembered, my dear?'

'It's not important,' Marina said. 'And I'm so sorry I interrupted your conversation.'

'That's all right, my dear. I'll pop down later in the week to see about a treatment, but we're off to the beach now,' she said. 'Come on.' she linked her arm through her husband's and off they went.

'It was Leanne,' Marina said, in a hushed tone.

'Leanne?'

'Yes. I'm certain of it. She tricked me into leaving her on her own in the salon and…'

'Are you the manager?' a voice said, from behind them.

Both Elena and Marina turned.

'Yes, Elena Lacey. How can I help?' Elena asked, plastering a smile on her face.

'We wanted twin beds and we've been put in a double. It's not good enough you know. This is supposed to be a four-star hotel and–'

'I'm sure that we can sort that out for you,' Elena said to the man before turning to Marina. 'Would you excuse me, Marina?'

'Of course, Elena. I'll come and find you when you've finished assisting the guest,' Marina said and disappeared into the hotel.

She returned to the spa and decided to shower and change, hoping that Elena would then be free to talk to her. She made her way up to reception when she'd finished and was told that Elena was in her office.

Marina hurried to Elena's office and was about to knock on the door. She hesitated as she realised that two voices were coming from inside. One of them was Leanne's.

'When you were with Stephen, did he ever lose his temper and threaten you in any way, Leanne?'

'He could be very impatient, and I haven't told anyone else but he does have a temper. Stephen is very spoilt and if he didn't get his own way, his reaction could be quite frightening.'

'Yet you were hoping to marry him?' Elena said, 'even though some of his behaviour frightened you?'

'I didn't mean it like that. It could be frightening for someone who didn't know how to handle him. Fortunately, I did. And anyway, I knew I could bring him around to my way of thinking and change him in time.'

'I thought I could change a man once, Leanne,' Elena said, 'and I can tell you without doubt that that road leads to disaster.'

'It doesn't matter now though, does it. Stephen's banged up for murder and my fairy tale wedding isn't going to happen.'

'I'm so sorry that this has happened to you, Leanne.'

Marina peeked her head around the door. Leanne didn't see her, but Elena did and she gave an imperceptible shake of her head, while Leanne wiped away a stray tear.

'Me too, Elena. But onwards and upwards eh? Was there anything else?'

'Yes. I wanted to talk to you about Marina's—'

'Hi, did I hear my name?' Marina said, walking into the office. 'I'm sorry to interrupt but can I talk to you in private, Elena, please.' She turned so Leanne couldn't see her face and gave Elena a warning look.

'Of course. Thanks, Leanne, there wasn't anything else.'

'But you–'

'We'll catch up another time, it wasn't important.'

Leanne hesitated as she looked from one to the other. Marina gave her a big smile, 'Awkward client,' she said. 'I really need Elena's help to sort this out.'

'Of course,' Leanne said, then left the office, not believing a word of it.

After Leanne had left the office, Marina closed the door, put a finger to her lips, and waited a few seconds. She opened it again and Leanne was still there.

'I've lost an earring,' Leanne said, as she bent to the floor to look. It was pretty obvious to Marina and Elena that she'd been trying to listen at the door.

'I'll help you,' Marina said.

'It's not there, Marina, I've looked. I must have dropped it on the way to Elena's office so I'll need to retrace my steps. I'd best get on.' And with that, she disappeared along the corridor.

Marina closed the door.

'What was that about?' Elena asked, now convinced that Leanne was no longer listening. 'And why would she want to eavesdrop on our conversation?'

'Guilt, Elena,' Marina said, as she closed the door. 'She came to book an appointment in the spa last Thursday. When I asked her how she was, she burst into tears and told me about breaking up with Stephen. She said that she'd been certain they would marry but he'd broken her heart by having an affair with an older, married woman. As well as blaming the woman, she also blamed the woman's husband for not being able to keep his own wife satisfied. She was distraught.'

'Go on.'

'I gave her some tissues and offered her a drink of water. She replied that she was in shock and that brandy would be better. She noticed me hesitate, then said that it was all right, and that she understood that I was busy and didn't have the time to talk to someone like her. I felt so awful I went up to the bar to get the brandy.'

'Even though she was on duty?'

'Yes, Elena. I felt sorry for the woman and it was what she wanted so I thought one small brandy wouldn't do any harm.'

'And where was Celia?'

'She'd just finished tidying the storeroom and was on her break before the next appointment. I was finishing later that day for the long weekend and Celia was going to cover.'

'Are you saying you believe that Leanne stole the Botox?'

'I think she did, yes. I can't prove it, Elena, but she seemed a lot better when I returned from the bar. Remarkably so, in fact. She knocked the brandy down in one, apologised for being emotional, and left shortly after without booking any appointments. She had a big handbag with her so could have put it in there, or even hidden it somewhere to collect later if there wasn't enough room in her bag.

'There's a chance I could lose my licence for not having looked after it properly. She might be counting on the fact that I wouldn't report it to the police. Or it might not be her—but the timings fit and I've checked and there weren't any other visitors prior to the Botox clinic.'

'I think we're taking a massive leap here. Leave this with me, Marina, until the police come and investigate. I can do my own digging around in the meantime.'

Marina's eyes widened. 'What do you mean by that?'

'I have contacts in the police and I can speak to them.'

'I want all this to be above board, Elena, so please be careful. The regulations on the storage and use of controlled substances are much stricter here than in many other countries. When the police do visit, they'll know that I reported it missing as soon as I discovered what happened, and that way I may just get a warning instead of being taken off the register as it's the first time that anything like this has happened to me here, or any other salon I've worked in for that matter.'

'Okay, that's a fair point. Like you said, we're not expecting the police to visit any time soon anyway. And it certainly will all be above board. Trust me, Marina, I wouldn't do anything to jeopardise your career, or mine, or to spoil the reputation of this hotel that I've worked extremely hard to build up. But I won't tolerate a thief in our midst either. I'll contact you as soon as I've got to the bottom of this, but in the meantime, don't say a word to anyone else.'

Marina reluctantly agreed to leave it for Elena to deal with until the police arrived, and returned to the spa, knowing it would be a struggle to concentrate on her appointments for the remainder of the day.

By the time they returned to the station it was midday and ten am in the U.K. While George went off to brief his team and took Chloe with him, Matt prepared himself for the video call that his former boss had arranged.

'You can use my office,' George said.

'Thanks, George. See you later.'

The big office was at the corner of the building and had loads of windows. Matt could see the hills in one direction and the sea in another. Tourists would pay a fortune for these spectacular views and Matt wondered how George could concentrate on work with such a beautiful distraction all around him. Through one set of glass doors, he could also see the open space where the other detectives beavered away. George would be able to tell which of his staff was in attendance without having to look through the booking in and out log.

He joined the call and had a quick chat with his boss before the Justice of the Peace joined. 'We decided that you should go first,' Dale said. 'They've delayed the kids for fifteen minutes, so we'd best get on.'

The kids were the other police officers; young men and women, starting out on their new careers. Although Matt knew he'd be working for the police again, he hadn't expected to have to swear the oath, but the Souvia Commissioner had decided that anyone working for his organisation had to either swear allegiance to their own country's force, or to his. The Justice of the Peace indicated that she was ready.

'I do solemnly and sincerely declare and affirm that I will well and truly serve the Queen in the office of constable, with fairness, integrity, diligence and impartiality…' Matt started. The words hadn't changed from almost thirty years ago, when he'd first read the declaration on that cold morning of his passing out parade. Matt had refreshed his memory of the words so that he didn't have to look at a piece of paper while he was on the call.

'Congratulations, Mr Elliott,' the JP said, once Matt had finished. 'And welcome back.'

'Thank you, Ma'am, Sir,' Matt said solemnly.

The JP left the call and Matt gave Dale a quick update on events before concluding the call.

'Good luck with this one, Matt,' Dale said. 'And let's check in twice a week unless anything significant happens in between. I'll get Penny to email you the details.'

They said their goodbyes, neither knowing that the case would be concluded almost before it had begun. When Matt left George's office, the main investigation room was quiet with all of the other detectives still in their meeting. He went to the desk he'd been allocated and saw a small black ID card holder next to the phone. Smiling to himself, he opened his Souvia Police ID. Impressed with their efficiency, he admired the badge.

The team started to filter back to their desks following the meeting and when Demitri Lambrou, the uniformed desk sergeant, heard what was going on, he went in search of Chloe.

'Ah, there you are,' he said, when he found her heading to the main investigation room. 'I might be able to save you a lot of time and leg work.'

Chloe could see he was almost bursting with news of something for her. 'What is it, Demi?'

'One of my guys took a call this morning from the boss of the beauty spa…,' He looked at the message. '…Marina's Sanctuary at the Griffon's Rest.'

'Marina Papadopolous?'

'That's right. Do you know her?'

'I do, yes. I've met her through my friend, Elena Lacey, who manages the Griffon's Rest.'

'Well, Marina said that she had a Botox clinic on Friday, but Celia, the girl who works for her, had to cancel it because, at the time, she'd thought there'd been a mix up in deliveries. Marina was off on a long weekend but since returning today and speaking to Celia, she discovered there was some sort of mix up. She said that the Botox was actually delivered but went missing. Although it's a regulated substance I didn't think much of it and told her we'd send someone around in due course–but now that we know Mr Green was poisoned by the exact same substance, we may have just found where it happened and be very close to discovering who did it too.'

'Brilliant, Demi. They were on my list to call later on today but you've saved me loads of time. Thanks! I could kiss you!'

'I don't think Mrs Lambrou would be very happy with that, Chloe,' the older sergeant said with a smile. 'Glad to be of assistance. Now go and see if you can catch our murderer before he or she decides to try it out on somebody else.'

Chloe thanked him again and went in search of her boss to keep him up to date with the developments. George was in a meeting briefing his boss, and Matt was familiarising himself with his desk and the software the Souvia police used to check on those with previous convictions of theft of poisonous substances.

'Excellent news,' Matt said, when Chloe told him about the missing Botox. He picked his phone and badge up from the desk and stood.

'I'm coming with you,' he said, when Chloe gave him a questioning look.

When Leanne was convinced that Marina had thought she'd returned to the kitchen, she doubled back and crept towards Elena's office. The corridor was quiet and she was able to pick up the gist of the conversation while also keeping her eyes open for any other movement along the corridor.

When she'd heard enough, Leanne slunk along the corridor, past reception and out of the hotel. She went around the back to the gardens and sat on the bench, planning her next move. Elena and Marina were onto her, and if she'd heard correctly, Marina had already reported the theft to the police. Leanne wasn't stupid and she knew it would only be a matter of time before she was arrested and charged with theft. And she'd heard there was to be a post-mortem that morning. Her warped mind told her that if Stephen hadn't decided to attack Rob Green, there wouldn't have been a post-mortem and nobody would have known about the poisoning, but now…

She took a packet of cigarettes and a lighter out of her pocket. She'd only started again since Stephen had ended it last Thursday and she, in turn, had decided to start her punishment of the people who had caused her fairy tale future to come tumbling down around her. She'd only just begun, and Leanne had no intention of letting Elena or Marina stop her from punishing the other guilty parties.

She reflected on Stephen for a moment. After all of her hard work finding him and getting him to fall for her, her life of luxury was over before it had even started. She'd now have to live from hand to mouth, working hard and barely surviving, while serving rich people who could afford holidays abroad and expensive rounds of golf – and that was only if she was lucky. When the post-mortem results were in, it wouldn't take a genius to put two and two together and to realise what had really happened. Leanne took a final drag of her cigarette and then stubbed it out on the ground. She put her hand in her other pocket, lifted out the vial and looked at it. Knowing what she had to do to save her skin, and so she could continue with her plan and eventually punish Fiona Green, she walked back to the front of the hotel with a new sense of purpose.

'Anyone seen Leanne Carter?' Elena asked the staff at the reception desk as soon as she'd finished dealing with a guest.

'Right behind you,' Leanne said.

Elena turned to face the front door as Leanne walked through it.

'I need to talk to you again, Leanne. Can you spare me a few minutes please?'

'Of course,' she said, following her boss, 'but before we talk, can you ask Marina to join us. I have something to tell you both.'

She's going to confess to the theft, Elena thought to herself. 'Okay. I'll call the spa,' she said, walking back to reception and picking up one of the internal phones.

Leanne listened to what she could, while appearing to those around her to be fascinated by what she was looking at on her mobile phone.

'Celia, is Marina there please? I need her to meet with me and Leanne. …I see. …No, don't do that, but tell her to call me as soon as she's finished.'

Elena put the phone down. 'She's doing a facial and then a full body massage and will be a little while. Go back to work and I'll give you a shout later, when Marina's free.'

'Oh that's a shame,' Leanne said, and nodded her head, indicating that Elena should follow her away from the reception area. The man and woman on reception pretended not to notice, but were adept at reading body language and watching without the watched knowing. Leanne was well aware of this and walked far enough away for them not to be able to hear, and still she spoke quietly. 'I may not be here later after you've heard what I need to tell you. Can we go somewhere private please, just you and me?'

Elena thought for a second before answering. Then her curiosity won out over her better judgement. 'Of course. The Flamingo Room. I'll tell them on reception that I'm not to be disturbed.'

'I'll get some refreshments while you do that, Elena. Coffee?'

'Just hot water with a slice of lemon for me, please.'

Leanne made her way to the kitchen. The lemon would be perfect.

Elena went to reception and asked for the key to the Flamingo Room which was on the first floor, next to the main conference room.

'I'm not to be disturbed please, unless it's a matter of life and death.'

She didn't realise at the time how profound her words would turn out to be.

As Elena waited for Leanne to join her with the refreshments, Matt and Chloe arrived at the hotel and made their way to Marina's Sanctuary. They were met by the smile of Celia at the welcome desk. They showed their badges; Chloe's as a full-time member of the Souvia Police Force, Matt's with a large 'S' for secondment, although members of the public only saw badges of office and wouldn't recognise the difference.

'We'd like to speak to Marina Papadopolous, please, regarding the theft of controlled substances.'

Celia gave her best smile. 'I'm sorry, that won't be possible at the moment. Marina's with a client and–'

'Interrupt her, please. This is very important,' Chloe said.

'But–'

'Now, please.'

Celia disappeared, and a few minutes later Marina appeared, a worried expression on her face, closely followed by her client.

'I'm so sorry for the inconvenience, Helena,' Marina said to the woman. 'Next week's appointment is on me, by way of apology.'

'It's all right, Marina, these things happen,' the client responded, appearing more interested in the two visitors.

'We're here to speak to Marina,' Matt said. 'We won't keep you.'

The woman took the hint and Marina waited until she had left before she spoke.

'Hello,' she said, without waiting for an answer. 'Do we have to do this now, Chloe? My business could be in ruins due to the theft and if my customers think I'm unreliable, I've got no chance.'

'We'll be as quick as we can be,' Chloe replied. 'And I'm sorry, Marina, but this is a serious investigation concerning more than theft, so it can't wait. Can you confirm that an amount of Botox was stolen from your Spa last Thursday?'

'Yes, I can, and I'm almost certain it was stolen by Leanne Carter.'

'We have reason to believe that the Botox was used to poison and kill someone,' Matt said. 'Is Leanne Carter one of your clients? It's important that we find her as soon as possible.'

'Others could be in danger,' Chloe added.

Celia was tidying up the treatment room but had been listening all of the time. 'That's easy,' she chirped as she walked towards them, used towels under one arm. 'Leanne's in a meeting with the manager. She phoned while you were in the treatment room, Marina, asking if you could join them, but I said you'd be a few hours and Elena said it could wait.'

'With Elena?' Matt asked.

'Yes. Is everything okay?'

Matt and Chloe didn't wait for an answer as they rushed to the lift. Marina and Celia looked at each other in alarm.

'Hold the fort,' Marina said, and chased after the detectives.

The lift doors were open and Chloe pressed the button for Reception, not waiting for Marina. As slow as it seemed, they both knew it was quicker than running along a corridor and up two sets of stairs.

'Elena Lacey,' Matt said, as soon as they arrived at the reception. 'Where is she?'

'In a meeting and she's asked not to be disturbed, Mr Elliott,' the receptionist said, and then turned her head towards Chloe. 'Something's wrong isn't it? Paul, look after things here–' She rushed around to the front of the long reception desk. 'Come with me.'

They followed her up the stairs towards the conference room.

'Who's with Elena?' Matt asked, in the hope that there'd been a mistake.

'Leanne Carter. Something funny's going on, but I'm not sure what. Here we are, the Flamingo Room.'

There was a stylish mural of one of the pretty birds on the wall outside the room, but Matt and Chloe took no notice as they burst into the room and took in the scene in front of them.

Elena and Leanne were sitting at a table opposite each other, and Elena had a cup, almost touching her lips.

'No, Elena,' Matt called, 'don't drink it!'

Leanne stood up at the same time that Matt shouted and she leaned over towards Elena. Matt figured she was going to try to force the cup into Elena's mouth. Without consciously thinking, he took a run and leap, knocking Leanne to the ground. Her chair went flying into the air and landed some distance away from her.

'Don't drink out of the cup!' Matt screamed at Elena, in case she hadn't got it the first time.

At the same time, Leanne jumped up to her feet, heading for the door, and escape.

'Jesus Christ, Matt, what the hell?' Elena gasped.

Matt noticed she'd put the cup down. Now that he knew she was safe, his main concern became stopping Leanne from making good her escape. He needn't have worried.

Chloe charged for the door but knew that Leanne would get out of the room before she reached her, unless she did something drastic. Taking her cue from Matt's actions a few seconds before, she took a run and leaped through the air. Chloe put her arms out as she did so and the distance between them disappeared. She rugby tackled Leanne, bringing her body to the floor.

'Ouch, gerroff,' Leanne protested, as she tried to drag herself towards the door, failing miserably as Chloe still had hold of her legs. 'This is police brutality! I'm going to sue you.'

'Shall we check to see what you've put in my cup first, Leanne?' Elena said sweetly.

Leanne knew she was caught and stopped moving. Not believing that the woman had given up that easily, Chloe jumped nimbly to her feet, taking out the handcuffs she carried in her back pocket as she did so. She bent over Leanne and grasped her two arms together; then she cuffed her, and pulled her onto her feet. While Matt held onto their suspect, Chloe took out her phone and made a quick call to the station.

The receptionist watched from the door, as did a small crowd who had heard the kerfuffle and come to check it out.

'If you'd kept your big noses out of it, nobody would have known any different,' said Leanne, 'and we all could have got on with our boring little lives.'

'Until the next time somebody upset you,' said Matt, 'and you decided they no longer deserved to have a boring little life. God only knows how many people you would have killed before we stopped you.'

'It's not like that. Rob Green was a spur of the moment decision.' Leanne was almost whinging now, like a child who'd been caught with their hand in the sweetie jar when their mother had told them they couldn't have any more.

'You killed him because your boyfriend was unfaithful to you, with his wife. That's hardly a spur of the moment decision, Leanne,' Elena said.

'Will you keep my job open for me?'

'What? Are you totally bonkers?'

'That's something that the jury will have to decide before locking me up, Elena,' Leanne said, her face now bearing a sinister smile.

Elena saw the evil in Leanne's eyes for the very first time and she shivered. It quickly dawned on her that she'd had a lucky escape, very lucky, and the woman standing in front of her appeared not to have any conscience.

'I've employed a psychopath,' she muttered to herself as much as to anyone else. Normally a good judge of character, Elena wondered how she had let herself take her eye off the ball to have employed a woman as evil as Leanne Carter. Not to mention her spoilt ex-boyfriend who also had it in him to snuff out a life without a second thought, whether by accident or design.

Chloe forced Leanne onto a chair and sat beside her. Marina arrived a few seconds later, along with a number of uniformed police, and George. As the uniformed officers took Leanne down to the station, George asked Chloe to take a statement from Marina. When he saw how distressed his cousin was, he was about to ask Matt to look after her, but saw that he already had it in hand, as he was holding Elena in his arms.

'Good job, you guys,' he said.

With Matt's arms around her, Elena felt instantly protected. She put her head on his shoulder as he moved them away from the others to a quiet corner of the room.

'You've had a shock,' he said. 'She'll be locked up for a very long time and won't bother you or anyone else, ever again. It's going to be all right, and you're going to be all right.'

'I thought I could catch her, Matt, and get a confession out of her. You know, help you guys out a bit.

It didn't occur to me for one moment that she would try to poison me, or Marina.'

Epilogue

Leanne Carter and Stephen Goodman were in prison in Souva, their trials due to take place the following month. Neither had been granted bail. Stephen's parents had paid for his legal defence but were now more determined than ever that he should stand on his own two feet.

Matt was returning to England that evening and was making the most of his last day with Elena. They were up at the crack of dawn and decided to start the day with a long, early morning walk along the beach.

'Just look at that,' Matt said, pointing towards the countryside in the East where the sun was starting its daily journey. Peeping over the hills, it cast its glow on the surrounding sky, changing the colours from night to day in a kaleidoscope of beautiful oranges, yellows, and pale reds. 'I'm going to miss this place so much.'

She smiled sadly and squeezed his hand as they continued their walk. 'Chloe told me about Leanne's parents when you guys went to search the house. About her father saying she was useless and her mother adding that she'd blown it again and would never marry anyone with money now. What chance did she have with parents like that?' Elena sighed. 'I don't even think that she loved Stephen, you know, she just wanted him for what she could get out of him.'

'Lots of people have issues with the way they've been brought up, Elena, but that doesn't turn them into murderers or psychopaths.'

'I suppose that's a fair point,' Elena acknowledged, nodding.

'And we know that Stephen didn't love her either, as according to the local gossip, he was pretty much smitten with Mrs Green.'

'And despite Mrs Green's protestations to the contrary,' Elena said, 'she clearly didn't love her husband enough to be faithful to him.'

'Mr and Mrs Goodman seem pretty solid though, Elena, but heartbroken that their only son is going to end up in prison. He's fortunate that he's only been charged with grievous bodily harm and not attempted manslaughter.'

'Well, he deserves to go to prison, and hopefully, it'll shock him into growing up and learning to look after himself. I trusted him and he was good at some parts of his job. But I didn't realise he was such a spoilt brat. He's in his mid-twenties for God's sake! Anyone would think he's a teenager by some of his actions; and a dangerous one at that.'

'I know what you mean, and it'll either make or break him. I'm not sure about Leanne though. Her defence will have a job trying to prove that she didn't mean to kill Rob Green. I didn't believe her, Elena, and if the jury feels the same, she'll be sentenced to life.'

'She deserves it, Matt. You know how I felt about Rob Green but that doesn't mean I wanted to see him dead. And killing someone because your boyfriend is sleeping with their wife is a bit bizarre, to say the least.'

'You never know what's going on in someone else's head, Elena. I've learned that over the years. Very little surprises me these days.'

'I hope I have the ability to surprise you, Matt?'

'You do, Elena, just about every day.'

She threw back her head and laughed, and he smiled, wishing he could bottle the feelings he had when he was with her.

'Here goes then,' she took a deep breath. 'I think you should leave your life in England, and come and live in Griffon Point.'

'That's hardly surprising, Elena, as we've already discussed it and agreed that's the long-term plan,' he said, and gave her a wry smile.

'Good grief, Matt, you sound like a solicitor or an accountant.'

'I do, do I?' Matt asked, with a twinkle in his eyes. He quickly grabbed Elena's waist with both hands and found the spot. She squealed as he started to tickle her, then she took off down the beach at a run. Matt followed and noticed an old couple walking towards them as he did so. Less than a minute later he caught up with Elena who was speaking to them in Greek. They stared at Matt in an unfriendly manner, until Elena said something and then each shook their head, said something to the other in Greek, and carried on with their walk.

'What was all that about?' he asked, trying to catch his breath after his short burst of running.

'They thought you were going to attack me.'

'I hope you told them I wasn't?'

Both laughing, they carried on walking.

'It's good that you didn't screw your face up when you were running, Matt. I take it your knee's okay?'

'I haven't had any pain in my joints since my second day here, Elena. The sun seems to be doing me the world of good.'

'And this is with our weather heading for winter, Matt. Just imagine how you'd feel at the height of the summer!'

'Drained and lethargic if it's as hot and sticky as I've heard people say it is.'

'Matt!' Elena said, her expression instantly changing from joy to despair.

'I think…' they both said at the same time, then laughed awkwardly.

'Go on.' Elena said.

'No, you go first.'

'I think you should come and live here,' Elena said.

Matt hesitated for a few moments, which she interpreted as bad news.

'I'm sorry, I thought you wanted the same. No need to feel awkward, we can just…'

'I do want the same, Elena. I want this more than I've wanted anything for a long time, a very long time in fact. So much so…'

'What? So much so what?'

'I have something to show you. But first, the good news is that I've booked my flight to come over, permanently.'

'Oh, Matt, that's great!' she said, flinging herself at him with such force that Matt toppled backwards and they ended up on the sand, with Elena on top of him.

'It's a good job my joints are all in working order!'

She rolled off him and leaned on an elbow, looking at him. Both were oblivious to the sand getting onto their clothes and skin.

'When are your flights? We need to sort out our living arrangements. Do you want to move in with me? We haven't really discussed that have we? I'd need to find a bigger place, especially as you're going to bring the dog with you. Do you think that…?'

'Let me know when I can get a word in,' Matt said, and she cuffed him playfully. 'The earliest I can get me and Jenny on the same flight is in two months, but this will give me time to get all my ducks in a row in England.'

'Two months, Matt! But that's ages away. We won't be together for Christmas either. Saying that, we're expecting a busy one and I'll be working.'

'I know it may seem like a long time but it'll fly by if you're busy. It will give me time to get everything sorted too, like renting my house and organising my business, which Keith wants to join. This is going to be for life, Elena, as far as I'm concerned.'

'Me too, Matt. But now that we've found each other, I don't want us to be apart.'

She climbed on top of him and they kissed, oblivious to the other people who were out on their early morning exercise.

'And our living arrangements?' she asked, when they came up for air.

Matt hoisted himself to his feet and pulled Elena up off the sand. They brushed as much of it off their clothes as they could.

'Let's make our way back to the car,' Matt said. 'I have something to show you…'

He loved the house he planned to rent, and hoped that Elena would feel the same way about it, too.

She held his hand, squeezing it tightly as they walked back along the beach, secure in the knowledge that as long as they had each other, they could tackle anything the world threw at them.

Acknowledgements

Thanks to my wonderful husband Allan, to my awesome editor Jill Turner, and to the uber talented Jessica Bell for another fantastic cover. Thanks also to all of my lovely friends for their support, especially Julie, Trudy, Su, Tina, Craig, Libby, Helen, Jo, Tania, Simon, Gail, and Sue.

Thank you for purchasing this book. If you have time to leave a short review so that other readers can find my books, I'd be extremely grateful.

Author's Note

If you enjoyed this you may like some of my other books:

The Island Dog Squad Book 1 (Sandy's Story)
Free at this link https://dl.bookfunnel.com/wdh6nl8p08
The Island Dog Squad Book 2 (Another Secret
Mission
The Island Dog Squad Book 3 (People
Problems)

Unlikely Soldiers Book 1 (Civvy to Squaddie)
Unlikely Soldiers Book 2 (Secrets and Lies)
Unlikely Soldiers Book 3 (Friends and Revenge)
Unlikely Soldiers Book 4 (Murder and Mayhem)

The Afterlife Series Book 1 (Beyond Death)
The Afterlife Series Book 2 (Beyond Life)
The Afterlife Series Book 3 (Beyond Destiny)
The Afterlife Series Book 4 (Beyond Possession)
The Afterlife Series Book 5 (Beyond Limits)
The Afterlife Series Book 6 (Beyond Sunnyfields)

Court Out (A Netball Girls' Drama)

Zak, My Boy Wonder (non-fiction)

And for children:

Jason the Penguin (He's Different)
Jason the Penguin (He Learns to Swim)

Reindeer Dreams

Further information is on my website https://debmcewansbooksandblogs.com or you can connect with me on Facebook: https://www.facebook.com/DebMcEwansbooksandblogs/?ref=bookmarks

About the Author

Following a career of almost thirty-five years in the British Army, Deb and her husband moved to Cyprus to become weather refugees.

She's written children's books about Jason the penguin and Barry the reindeer and young adult/adult books about dogs, soldiers, and netball players, as well as a non-fiction book about a boy born to be different. Her most popular books are the supernatural suspense Afterlife series which was inspired by ants. Deb was in the garden contemplating whether to squash an irritating ant or to let it live and wondered whether anyone *up there* decides the same about us and thus the series was born.

The first book in the Unlikely Soldiers series is set in nineteen-seventies Britain. The second covers the early eighties and includes the Falklands War, service in Northern Ireland and (the former) West Germany. 'Friends and Revenge' is the third in the series and takes a sinister turn of events. 'Murder and Mayhem' is the final book of the series and takes our heroine from the former West Germany, to London and to an action-packed Hong Kong.

'Court Out (A Netball Girls' Drama)' is a standalone novel. Using netball as an escape from her miserable home life, Marsha Lawson is desperate to keep the past buried and to forge a brighter future. But she's not the only one with secrets. When two players want revenge, a tsunami of emotions is released at a tournament, leaving destruction in its wake. As the wave starts spreading throughout the team, can Marsha and the others escape its deadly grasp, or will their emotional baggage pull them under, with devastating consequences for their families and team-mates?

'Zak, My Boy Wonder', is a non-fiction book co-written with Zak's Mum, Joanne Lythgoe. Deb met Jo and her children when she moved to Cyprus with Allan in 2013. Jo shared her story over a drink one night and Deb was astounded, finding it hard to believe that a family could be treated with such cruelty, indifference and a complete lack of compassion and empathy. This sounded like a tale from Victorian times and not the twenty-first century. When Deb suggested she share her story, Jo said she was too busy looking after both children – especially Zak who still needed a number of surgeries – and didn't have the emotional or physical energy required to dig up the past. Almost fourteen years later, Jo felt ready to share this harrowing but inspirational tale of a woman and her family who refused to give up and were determined not to let the judgemental, nasty, small-minded people grind them down.

'The Island Dog Squad' is a series of novellas inspired by the rescue dog Deb and Allan adopted in 2018. The real Sandy is a sensitive soul, not quite like her fictional namesake, and the other characters are based on Sandy's real-life mates.

Deb loves spending time with her husband Allan and rescue dog Sandy. She also loves writing, keeping fit, and socialising, and does her best to avoid housework.

Printed in Great Britain
by Amazon